Anonymous

Memorial Addresses on the Life and Character of Isham G. Harris

Second Edition

Anonymous

Memorial Addresses on the Life and Character of Isham G. Harris
Second Edition

ISBN/EAN: 9783337116293

Printed in Europe, USA, Canada, Australia, Japan

Cover: Foto ©Raphael Reischuk / pixelio.de

More available books at **www.hansebooks.com**

MEMORIAL ADDRESSES

ON THE

LIFE AND CHARACTER

OF

ISHAM G. HARRIS

(LATE A SENATOR FROM TENNESSEE),

DELIVERED IN THE

SENATE AND HOUSE OF REPRESENTATIVES,

FIFTY-FIFTH CONGRESS,
SECOND SESSION.

————————

WASHINGTON:
GOVERNMENT PRINTING OFFICE.
1898.

CONTENTS.

	Page.
Proceedings in the Senate	5
Memorial address by—	
Mr. BATE	14
Mr. MORRILL	29
Mr. MORGAN	33
Mr. HOAR	36
Mr. WALTHALL	39
Mr. HAWLEY	43
Mr. COCKRELL	44
Mr. STEWART	49
Mr. CHILTON	51
Mr. TURLEY	56
Speech of Hon. DAVID TURPIE, at Memphis, Tenn.	61
Proceedings in the House	71
Memorial address by—	
Mr. McMILLIN	73
Mr. BLAND	81
Mr. RICHARDSON	84
Mr. MEYER	89
Mr. McRAE	94
Mr. BENTON	96
Mr. RHEA	103
Mr. BROWNLOW	105
Mr. CLARKE	116
Mr. SIMS	118
Mr. DE ARMOND	124
Mr. GAINES	130
Mr. CARMACK	132
Mr. HARTMAN	140
Mr. SULZER	142
Mr. COX	170
Mr. KING	173
Appendix—	
Memorial ceremonies	148

DEATH OF ISHAM G. HARRIS.

PROCEEDINGS IN THE SENATE.

JULY 9, 1897.

Mr. BATE. Mr. President, it becomes my painful duty this morning to announce to the Senate the death of my colleague, and as a mark of respect I shall at the proper time make a motion for an adjournment, and will at some future time ask that a day be set apart specially for tributes to be delivered by Senators on his life and character.

A conspicuous figure. Mr. President, and a familiar one, identified as an active and influential factor in the history of this Chamber and of the country, is no longer one of us. ISHAM GREEN HARRIS for more than twenty years sat in this Chamber as a Senator from Tennessee, and for the last ten years it has been my honor and pleasure to be associated with him as his colleague. He died last evening at his residence in sight of this Capitol at an advanced age; an age, however, which he ever kept green and bright and buoyant until prostrated by his recent illness. Tennessee and the entire country mourn his loss.

The individual man and his personal characteristics are abundantly known to Senators who surround me, as they are to Tennesseeans and to the general constituency. He closed last evening a long career of usefulness to the country, especially to

5

his native State of Tennessee, which honored him with her highest official gifts and in turn has been honored by him.

He was a man of ideas, with high qualities of leadership and statesmanship, with courage to assert and ability to maintain them. His devotion to duty, as he conceived it, and its faithful and fearless discharge inspired confidence and friendship, while it often disarmed opposition. The benefit of his ripe experience and extended information as to the affairs of government is lost to us. His familiarity with parliamentary usage and his preeminence as a presiding officer make his loss the more keenly felt by the Senate. His honest, earnest, and incisive mode of debate and his ready, emphatic, and accurate manner of deciding questions, as presiding officer, will not pass away, but will live in the memory of Senators and in the history of the country.

Mr. President, Senator HARRIS belonged to that class of historic characters in this country known as "war governors." He is the last but one of that class upon either side, North or South, who took an active participation and presided over a sovereign State during that interstate struggle.

He was not, because he was governor, an active Confederate soldier in its strictest sense; but all his nature and all his sympathies were enlisted upon the Confederate side.

He was the governor of a strong and mighty State which furnished numbers of troops for the Confederate cause. They were organized under his administration. He could not, being governor of the State, enter the ranks or be sworn into the service by enlistment. He could not take that course, but nevertheless he was a live, active, influential factor in all that concerned the movement of Tennessee and of the Confederacy in that great war. He was present and as voluntary aid took part in all our great battles.

His life has been an eventful one, his history a noted one, and it will live after him. I need not speak of him here in this Chamber. Those who surround me knew him and understood his peculiarities, his personalities. He had them, and he had them in a generous way, and he always exercised them with a proper feeling and in a generous manner.

We may forget many things that transpired here, and some characters who have gone the way that he has gone; but, Mr. President, Senators will not forget the peculiar manner of expression that belonged to him, with his clear, straightforward, direct, and incisive speech on all occasions, without deviation. No man ever misunderstood what he meant, and no one will forget that peculiar emphasis which was his. Neither will any one in this Senate forget that promptness and readiness with which he always decided questions when he was in the chair. Such was his history here, and it will not only live in our memories, but it will belong to the political history of this country.

But he is gone. He is no longer one of us. On yesterday evening the summons came. The clouds seemed to surround him. All his nature, as it were, his past life, came before me when I understood that he was dying. I remembered him in my young manhood when he was first governor of Tennessee. I remembered him later on as the Confederate war governor of my State, when he heard the first reveille and the last tattoo in Confederate camps. I remembered him through the good and evil fortune of our Southland, ever vigilant and ready to further the cause he had espoused—and that his cause was my cause—and in his dying hour my pulse beat a warm sympathy and my heart went out in reverence for the grand old veteran.

But he is gone. Yesterday evening, a few minutes before 6 o'clock, the summons came. The shadows of death spread over him as a dark cloud; the curfew tolled the knell of his departing day; the soothing sound of "taps" invited sleep to the worn and weary veteran; he entered his silent tent; he sleeps there now on Fame's eternal camping ground.

Mr. President, I shall move to adjourn at the proper time, but meanwhile I will ask for the consideration of the resolutions which I send to the desk to be read.

The VICE-PRESIDENT. The resolutions submitted by the Senator from Tennessee will be read.

The resolutions were read, as follows:

Resolved, That the Senate has heard with profound sorrow of the death of the Hon. ISHAM G. HARRIS, late a Senator from the State of Tennessee.

Resolved, That a committee of nine Senators be appointed by the Vice-President to take order for superintending the funeral of Mr. HARRIS, which shall take place in the Senate Chamber at 12 o'clock m. to-morrow, and that the Senate will attend the same.

Resolved, That, as a further remark of respect entertained by the Senate for his memory, his remains be removed from Washington to Tennessee in charge of the Sergeant-at-Arms, and attended by the committee, who shall have full power to carry this resolution into effect.

Resolved, That the Secretary communicate these proceedings to the House of Representatives and invite the House of Representatives to attend the funeral in the Senate Chamber, and to appoint a committee to act with the committee of the Senate.

The resolutions were considered by unanimous consent, and agreed to.

The Vice-President appointed as the committee under the second resolution, Mr. Bate, Mr. Walthall, Mr. Berry, Mr. Turpie, Mr. Allen, Mr. Deboe, Mr. Pettus, Mr. Chilton, and Mr. Wetmore.

Mr. Cockrell submitted the following resolution; which was considered by unanimous consent, and agreed to:

Resolved, That invitations be extended to the President of the United States and the members of his Cabinet, the Chief Justice and associate justices of the Supreme Court of the United States, the diplomatic corps (through the Secretary of State), the Major-General commanding the Army, and the senior Admiral of the Navy to attend the funeral of the Hon. ISHAM G. HARRIS, late a Senator from the State of Tennessee, in the Senate Chamber at 12 o'clock meridian to-morrow.

Mr. Cockrell submitted the following resolution; which was considered by unanimous consent, and agreed to:

Resolved, That the expenses incurred by the select committee appointed to take order for the funeral of the late Senator ISHAM G. HARRIS be paid from the contingent fund of the Senate, upon vouchers to be approved by the chairman of said committee.

Mr. BATE. Mr. President, I move, as a further mark of respect to the memory of my deceased colleague, that the Senate do now adjourn.

The motion was unanimously agreed to; and (at 12 o'clock and 15 minutes p. m.) the Senate adjourned until to-morrow, Saturday, July 10, 1897, at 12 o'clock meridian.

FUNERAL OF SENATOR ISHAM G. HARRIS.

JUNE 10, 1897.

Rev. HUGH JOHNSTON, D. D., Acting Chaplain of the Senate, offered the following prayer:

Let us pray. Almighty God, Thou rulest the armies of heaven and among the children of men, according to Thy good pleasure, and none can stay Thine hand or say to Thee, What doest Thou? But though infinitely great, Thou art unspeakably good. Thou carest for us. We can not weep the tear Thou dost not see, or feel the pain Thou dost not know, or breathe the prayer Thou dost not hear, for Thy tender mercies are over all Thy works.

We thank Thee for life with all its blessings; for all the generations of men who have come and gone, and have sown and reaped and made for us such harvests of comfort and culture. We bless Thee that Thou dost not confine us to this present existence, but that after the training and discipline of life Thou dost open to us the gates of a second life, even the life that is immortal.

We give Thee thanks for the long and valuable service which the great statesman whose name has so suddenly become a memory was enabled to render to his country and to his State, for his rare qualities of leadership in the councils of the nation, for his sturdiness of purpose, and for those tender personal characteristics which so endeared him to his kindred and friends. We beseech Thee to comfort all who mourn. We entreat Thee give to his sons a firm trust in Thee and a tranquil submission to Thy will.

And here in this Chamber, where he was so conspicuous a personality, the scene of so many achievements and successes in public life, give Thy servants before Thee to see, give us all to see, how Thou dost level to the dust all distinctions of rank and station and honor, and that nothing endures but the fine gold of true character.

Help us, we beseech Thee, to build up manhood in Christ Jesus, to put our trust more firmly in that blessed and only Saviour who has died for our sins, who has conquered death, who has achieved a victory over the grave, and who opens the kingdom of heaven to all believers. To whom, with Thee and the Holy Ghost, be all honor and glory, world without end. Amen.

The VICE-PRESIDENT. Senators, by order of the Senate the usual business will be suspended this day to enable the Senate to participate in the funeral ceremonies deemed appropriate upon the death of ISHAM G. HARRIS, late an honored member of this body from the State of Tennessee. The reading of the Journal will be dispensed with.

At five minutes past 12 o'clock the members of the House of Representatives entered the Senate Chamber. The Chaplain of the House was escorted to a seat at the Secretary's desk, and the members of the House were shown to the seats on the floor provided for them. They were soon followed by members of the diplomatic corps, the President and his Cabinet ministers, the committee of arrangements of the two Houses, and members of the family of the deceased Senator, who were respectively escorted to the seats assigned them on the floor.

The burial service of the Methodist Episcopal Church was read by Rev. Hugh Johnston, D. D., assisted by Rev. J. W. Duffey, D. D., of the Methodist Episcopal Church South.

The benediction was pronounced by Rev. H. N. Couden, Chaplain of the House of Representatives.

The VICE-PRESIDENT. The funeral ceremonies are now terminated. The body of our late brother will now be committed to the charge of the officers of the Senate and to the committee representing the two Houses, to be conveyed to his late home in Tennessee, there to be buried among his family and friends.

Mr. BATE. Mr. President, I move that the Senate do now adjourn.

The motion was agreed to: and at 12 o'clock and 30 minutes p. m., the Senate adjourned until Monday, July 12, 1897, at 12 o'clock meridian.

MEMORIAL ADDRESSES ON THE LATE SENATOR HARRIS.

MARCH 24, 1898.

Mr. BATE. Mr. President, the hour set apart for the Senatorial ceremonies in memory of my late colleague, Senator HARRIS, has arrived, and I offer the resolutions which I send to the desk.

The PRESIDING OFFICER (Mr. Pasco). The resolutions submitted by the Senator from Tennessee will be read.

The Secretary read the resolutions, as follows:

Resolved, That the Senate has heard with profound sorrow of the death of Hon. ISHAM G. HARRIS, late a Senator from the State of Tennessee.

Resolved, That, as a mark of respect to the memory of the deceased, the business of the Senate be now suspended to enable his associates to pay proper tribute of regard to his high character and distinguished public services.

Resolved, That the Secretary communicate these resolutions to the House of Representatives.

Resolved, That as an additional mark of respect, the Senate, at the conclusion of these ceremonies, do adjourn.

The PRESIDING OFFICER. The question is on agreeing to the resolutions.

The resolutions were unanimously agreed to.

13

ADDRESS OF MR. BATE.

Mr. BATE. Mr. President, to my late distinguished colleague on this floor all the honors due to the most illustrious citizen have been paid by the officials of Tennessee and by the spontaneous affection of the citizens of the State. His body, by general and public request, lay in state in the capitol of Tennessee, escorted and guarded by old ex-Confederate soldiers, who stood sentinel around his bier under the two flags—Confederate and Federal.

The memorial services on a later day at Memphis, the home of the late Senator HARRIS, were of that character which attest the love and esteem in which he was held by the people of Tennessee. On that occasion the drapery of woe gave place to the beauty of flowers, and the vast auditorium bloomed and blossomed with the festoons of smilax and chrysanthemums, while palms of ancient and sacred memory vied with roses in giving grace and beauty to a scene which bore evidence of a purpose on the part of the whole community to unite in a grand testimonial to the honored dead.

Representative men, the rich and the poor, were there, and every creed in religion as well as every division in politics united in one testimonial to the memory of the citizen, the "war governor," and statesman who had passed away. Nothing which affection could suggest or pride propose was omitted by that community which he had served and in which he had so long resided.

The glimmer of the old gray uniform on the Confederate veterans on this memorial occasion recalled the glory of the past without in the least derogating from the duties of the present. He had worn that uniform with honor in the camp, on the

march, on the battlefield, and it was appropriate that a conspicuous place should be filled by it in the memorial service of
his past life. The proud emblems of the Federal Union were
not absent, but floated gracefully along with the modest little
ensign that bore the cross of St. Andrew, with its stars and bars.

It was a fit occasion for intertwining the two flags, and it was
tastefully and gracefully done. Notwithstanding these honors
so profusely paid by the authorities of Tennessee and of the city
of Memphis and of all classes of the people, an honored custom
of this Senate invites further posthumous ceremonies within its
historic walls which have so often reverberated his voice. This
Chamber for more than twenty years was the theater of his usefulness, the same in which he played that conspicuous part in
the public history which will be forever associated with his
memory. It is appropriate that here, then, in this Chamber
official recognition of his prominent services to the Union and to
the State should have voice and recognition.

I ask the attention of Senators while I briefly relate the story
of a man—their fellow—who is gone.

Mr. President, ISHAM GREEN HARRIS was born in Franklin
County, Tenn., on the 10th of February, 1818, and died in this
city on the 8th of July, 1897, having attained the ripe age of 80
years, fulfilling the words of the psalmist that "the days of our
years are threescore years and ten; and if by reason of strength
they be fourscore years, yet is their strength labor and sorrow;
for it is soon cut off, and we fly away."

Little did the neighbors and friends of the Harris family, who
lived in an unostentatious but independent way among the plain
and patriotic people of Franklin County, Tenn., dream that on
the 10th of February, 1818, there was born in their midst a
child who was destined to be a leading factor in stirring events
that were to come to our country's history—one who was to

organize troops to fight great battles—was three times to occupy the executive chair of our great State and sit twenty years in the chief council chamber of our great country as one of its advisers and leaders. There was no special announcement of his birth by the parents or any special recognition of it given by the neighbors or the church. It nevertheless was one that has gone into history and will live beyond the present generation into the far future.

Isham and Lucy Harris, the father and mother of this the youngest of nine children, were North Carolinians and of Revolutionary stock. Isham's grandfather was an officer in the Revolutionary war. The father and mother, leaving the Old North State, seeking fresher fields in which to better their fortunes, journeyed westward over the mountains and settled where the waters of Elk River flow through a beautiful valley overlooked by the western range of the Cumberland Mountains. It was here, on a farm in Franklin County, Tenn., that these pioneer parents in a plain and frugal way reared and educated their children.

The log-house home and country schoolhouse were familiar features in that day, and to-day Tennessee points to them, through the brightest pages of her history, with greater pride than can any king point to his palace or any scholar to his university alma mater, for these unpretending homes and schools were the sources of that great intellectual, moral, and political strength that made heroes and statesmen of her sons and gave an unsurpassed charm to her womanhood.

But this monotonous and narrow sphere of social and business life, though with many attractions, was too circumscribed for young ambition to vault itself, and the subject of this tribute, at the early age of 14, with only a country-school education, full of manhood and self-reliance, with a heart throbbing with

courageous impulses and a brain restless and full of resources—
this boy-man, ISHAM GREEN HARRIS, with the consent and
blessing of his father, for whom he was named, launched his
little lifeboat, freighted with his hopes and fortune, on the
uncertain sea of the future.

Leaving home at this unripe age, he went west to Paris,
Henry County, Tenn., which became his future home. By way of
being independent of the assistance of friends, he hired himself
as a merchant's clerk, beginning at the bottom with a small salary.
By strict attention to business, performing every duty with alac-
rity and guided by that conspicuous executive ability that characterized all his life, he soon found himself at the head of an
establishment of his own and conducted it with eminent success.

After having undergone varied fortune in the commercial line,
meantime having matured into manhood, he entered upon the
profession of the law, and soon showed his aptness in and his
adaptability to his profession. But while he was successful in
securing a clientage and was strict in attention to the business
intrusted to him, he was dreaming of the future, and saw, as in
an apocalyptic vision, another field of service in which distinction
united with destiny.

His taste and capacity fitted him preeminently for this new
field, and his natural political sagacity and patriotic fervor beck-
oned him on. The gate opened its portals, and ambition, as a
seductive siren, drew him in her charmed circle of delirium as
naturally as iron filings are drawn to loadstone. Henceforth
the political field was to him most congenial, and it became the
arena in which was performed the life drama of ISHAM GREEN
HARRIS. Six years of successful practice of law brought unto
him not only a handsome income but established for him a
reputation as a lawyer, and more especially as an advocate.
This threw him actively into the political world, and in 1847

he was honored with a seat in the senatorial branch of the Tennessee legislature.

There his aptitude for successful management in political matters entitled him to leadership, which brought him so conspicuously before the public as a Democrat that in 1848 he was selected as the Democratic elector for the Ninth Congressional district, to be followed in 1849 by his election from that district to the United States House of Representatives. After serving that district through two successive Congresses, and being renominated the third time, he declined to accept the nomination and moved to Memphis, where he was recognized as a lawyer and advocate of ability, and as such took high rank at that bar, then, as now, distinguished for the ability of its members.

But political preferment and leadership being his ruling passion, and politics being the natural field for the exercise of his fine powers, he again, in 1856, came to the front as elector at large for the Democratic party. Those who recall that exciting political campaign and the issues involved, and remember that his immediate opponent was the able and distinguished Governor Neil S. Brown, a foeman worthy of any man's steel, will recognize it as a gladiatorial contest between evenly matched knights, and which attracted the attention of the whole State.

His speeches on the hustings were plain, clear, and cogent, severely without ornament, and no strain at eloquence or display, but always sensible, strong, attractive, and sometimes dramatic. In delivery he was earnest and forcible, and alike emphatic in expression and gesture. Indeed, this grew upon him with age until the emphatic seemed the dogmatic. In speaking he always had a definite point to drive to, and he let you know what it was, and generally got there in good time and in good order.

With the triumph of his party in that campaign, Tennessee

took rank among Democratic States, and his rich reward was a nomination and election, in 1857, as governor of the State. In this, his first canvass for governor, he had for his opponent Hon. Robert Hatton, the nominee of the opposing party, who was young, active, and talented, and it being the custom of Tennessee to have joint discussions between opposing party candidates, they canvassed the State together. HARRIS was elected. He was renominated in 1859, with John Netherland, a bright, talented man and famous stump orator, as his opponent. HARRIS was again elected.

His third election as governor was in August, 1861, after the State had united her fortunes with the Southern States and war was flagrant. Under the constitution of Tennessee the governor is elected for a term of two years, and remains in office until his successor is inaugurated, and this inauguration is required to be at the capitol and in the presence of the legislature. At the expiration of HARRIS's third term the capitol was within the Federal lines—hence there could be no inauguration, and HARRIS held over to the end of the war.

These renominations and successful canvasses show the hold he had gained and retained in the confidence and affection of the people of the whole State. His three canvasses for governor, together with performing the duties of the office, brought out those remarkable traits of character which made him conspicuous among the leaders of his party. He had by nature fine executive ability, which was strengthened by culture and habit. This executive quality was aided by an unflagging energy, which in turn was driven by a force of will that often overcame obstacles that were hard to remove.

Along with those, he had another gift or quality that was in evidence all along his line of life, and which contributed largely to his success. It is a species of diplomacy called in common parlance "tact;" that is he instinctively knew better when and how to accomplish an object than other men. This was to a great extent the result of his thorough and accurate knowledge of human nature. His great lever power, however, that sustained him in seeking official preferment and maintaining himself was his Jeffersonian faith in the people—faith in their doing right when the right is understood by them—and his undeviating adherence to what he believed to be their rights and interests.

Governor HARRIS belonged to the strict-construction school of politics. That school of construction was originated by Jefferson and Madison as a counterpoise to the growing tendency of Federal consolidation and as a force to bring back the Government from the centralization of the alien and sedition acts to the original object of its creation, the Federal agent of the sovereign States that created it.

It was afterwards illustrated by the genius of Calhoun and adorned with the abilities and virtues of Southern statesmen, and for many years had a grasp upon the people of the South which only the mailed hand of fratricidal war could tear away.

To that school of construction Governor HARRIS conscientiously attached himself.

Whatever others may think of that theory of our Government, to ISHAM G. HARRIS it was the gospel of his politics, the creed that formulated his political convictions, and to it he was as true as the needle to the pole.

State sovereignty and its resultant, the right of secession, were with him conscientious convictions, as sacred and binding as his belief in human existence. As governor it was his duty to take care that the State suffer no detriment, and to that end, when trouble and danger were in sight, he summoned the legislature in extra session, that a convention of the people of the State might take such action as their wisdom should dictate. It would serve no good purpose to review in this place the able messages in which he discussed the public conditions, the attitude of sections, and the ultimate purposes of political parties.

It is sufficient to say that he was no fanatic, but a calm, resolute, earnest, and honest man in a place of great responsibility; and with the courage of his convictions he met the public conditions by which his State was menaced with the only remedy that was provided in the theory of Federal Union as he understood that theory. Yea, many will say he and those of us who sustained him were wrong; but there can be none who knew him as I and those who stood by him in that great crisis did who can truthfully assert that he was not honest in his convictions and earnest in his work.

In the days of 1861 public events shaped themselves with a rapidity and suddenness which it is difficult to comprehend now, and not edifying to review on this floor. There is one incident, however, that occurred at this juncture between the governor of Tennessee and the President of the United States that can not with propriety be omitted in giving the leading features of Governor HARRIS's life.

Excitement for weeks over the whole country had been intense, and culminated in the fall of Fort Sumter, whereupon President Lincoln called for 75,000 troops to coerce the seceded States, and in the call designated two regiments to come from Tennessee, and asked Governor HARRIS to furnish them. The reply was promptly returned by the governor of Tennessee to the President in the following words:

Tennessee will not furnish a single man for the purpose of coercion, but 50,000, if necessary, for the defense of our rights and those of our Southern brethren.

There are many personal and official incidents connected with Governor HARRIS that would be interesting to know, but I forbear giving them, except the following one, illustrative of his high appreciation of the duty of an official in caring for the public interest intrusted to him: There was a large sum of money, nearly a million dollars in gold, in the custody of the State, known as "the school fund," when, on the approach of the Federal Army to the capitol of Tennessee, Governor HARRIS had this fund, among other effects of the State, sent south. He regarded it as a sacred fund, and on no account would permit it to be used. Under his orders it was moved from place to place as military lines shifted, and kept secure. When war scenes were dissolving and he going into exile, he directed its honest keepers to return it to the State authorities, which was done without the loss of a dollar.

It is my purpose only to present Governor HARRIS in his true character, that of a resolute, firm man, discharging every duty from a high sense of responsibility to the State and her people, indifferent to every personal consequence and solicitous only for the safety of the State and the protection of her people. To that end, when all hopes of continued peace vanished before the President's call for troops to invade the Southern States, Governor HARRIS bent every energy of his character and exerted every resource of the State to the organization and equipment of her volunteers; and so well did he work in those precarious days that by July, 1861, he had organized and equipped thousands of troops, turning them over to the Confederate authorities.

He relaxed no effort in the defense of the State, but with untiring energy continued his efforts to place the State in a condition to be defended by her own people as well as by the armies of the Confederate States. His example as governor was inspiring to all the people, infusing energy everywhere and bringing order out of confusion, until under his administration, which was during the entire war, over 100,000 Tennessee soldiers, as gallant and patriotic troops as ever mustered under battle flag, had enlisted and had been as well equipped as could be under the existing conditions and completely organized in the armies of the Confederate States, and thus he earned the well merited, and to him the most highly prized, sobriquet of the "War Governor of Tennessee."

When driven by the events of the war from the State and it was no longer possible for him to discharge the duties of the exalted office, he rested not, nor sought easy berth, but immediately entered the field on the staff of Gen. Albert Sidney Johnston, and was with him on the field of Shiloh and personally assisted that great chieftain at the time he received his death shot.

With the Army of Tennessee, under all its commanders, he served through all the years of the war, exerting every effort to mitigate the hardships of the soldiers, to supply the necessities of their daily life, and sharing with them the sunshine and the storm, the heat and the cold, the joy of victory and the sting of defeat.

Though not technically in the Confederate army, for he could not be, as he was governor of Tennessee, but he was in fact its inseparable companion from beginning to end, and heard its first reveille and its last tattoo. He was emphatically the friend of the soldiers, and omitted nothing that could contribute to their comfort or increase their efficiency. After the war, with all its disappointments, losses, and distress, the people of Tennessee still treasure in their hearts the sacred memory of their heroic soldiers.

> When all the blandishments of life are gone,
> * * * the brave live on.

All else seemed gone, under the inscrutable wisdom of an all-wise Providence, but the manhood of those four years. In all the noblest acceptation of that word, it is a precious heirloom to Confederates, to be transmitted from sire to son. Of that manhood Governor HARRIS was a living example, in its administrative feature, in its brave devotion to duty, in its unselfish attention to the wants of others, and in its bravery and endurance on the field of battle, and also in exacting demands in bivouac, march, and hospital.

The history of ISHAM G. HARRIS is inseparably connected with our war period. He was then in the prime of life and in the zenith of his power. He was governor during the entire time, from 1861–65, of a sovereign State, mighty in those effective elements of war, men and resources. It was an ill-starred destiny that came upon our country and brought a four-years carnival of suffering and death.

When the bloodshot eye of Mars looked down upon the scene, it was "red with uncommon wrath," and the smile of mercy appeased it not. Ours was then a land of armed men, brothers fighting each other. Destruction and death was the order of the day. Every march was to a battlefield, and every battlefield was a graveyard. Defeat of to-day gave earnest of victory to-morrow, while victory to-morrow meant defeat the next day. It was a struggle between giants, as fierce and unrelenting as that between Saracen and Crusader over the Holy Sepulcher when the battle-ax of Cœur de Lion found its death-producing counterpart in the magic blade of Saladin.

It was in these times that the subject of this tribute was at the helm, steering a mighty State through the crimson tide of war. But with peace there came not rest to his weary spirit. The triumph of the Union Army admitted of no magnanimity for him. The fierce passions of politics interposed to drive him into exile. The trumped-up charge of treason to the State, the State he had so courageously defended, was set in motion, and, with a reward for his capture, he was driven to seek safety in Mexico and there await a returning sense of shame to his persecutors.

From Mexico to England was for him a change from enforced idleness to that business activity so necessary to his energetic and ever-working nature. One year in business in Liverpool completed the two and a half years of exile, during which all charges were abandoned and rewards withdrawn, and he was free to return to the State and people he had served so faithfully and loved so well. A period of eight years followed with a successful practice of the law, during which the clouds of political animosities were being gradually dispelled and the people had become free to exercise their right of selecting their Representatives and Senators.

Governor HARRIS became a candidate and was elected by the legislature to the Senate of the United States, where, from 1877 to 1897, a period of over twenty years, he was the zealous and faithful ambassador of Tennessee to this Amphictyonic Council of sovereign States.

This Senate too well remembers my colleague for me to recall the weighty words, the impressive manner, the forcefulness in colloquy, the ready retort, the executive ability, tact, and discretion, the parliamentary management, the courtesy that ever characterized him in the chair—for he had been chosen its temporary presiding officer—the firmness with which he maintained his convictions, and the triumph he won.

His was a green and fresh old age. His eyes were not dim and lusterless, nor was his natural force much abated. He was never a better or more useful Senator nor more attentive and efficient to his duties than in the later years of his life. Age seemed only to have brought ripened experience with its advantages which he made available.

He was generally in his seat and always a watcher, even in weary nights when obstructive legislation was rampant. When younger men were inattentive and sought sleep, he, regardless of age, was awake and vigilant and ready for any turn in the game of political diplomacy that was going on, and generally took on such occasions a leading and effective part in all discussions pertaining to the rules of the Senate and parliamentary proceedings. Indeed he felt, and it came to be so regarded in the Senate, that debate on parliamentary proceedings was *his* fight, for he was the admitted authority on parliamentary law in the body.

Mr. President, Governor HARRIS lived in an eventful age. No eighty years of human action has brought to light so many useful discoveries and such great results. The map of the world has been changed during the period of his life. Empires have appeared and passed away like bubbles on the surface of the lake.

Continents that were comparatively vacant have become the abode of powerful States, peopled by intelligent inhabitants that enjoy all the advantages of a high civilization. At his birth this Republic was all east of the Mississippi; at his death the tide of population had crossed the Rocky Mountains and built powerful States and splendid cities on the Pacific. What at his birth was the American desert has become the abode of freemen, and enterprising communities now cheer the dreary wastes.

No railroad was then found on this continent, nor was it traversed by thousands of miles in which the traveler scales the lofty mountains and passes over the great rivers in splendid parlor cars, where his meals are served and he reposes on his downy bed while he spins along over wonderful scenery at the rate of 40 miles an hour. At his birth no scientist dreamed that each day's proceedings would be distributed through the world with a speed that far outstrips the earth in her daily revolutions around her axis. Yet the lightning has become the great agent of humanity to distribute its messages, propel its cars, and heat its habitations. The telephone is the faithful agent that repeats the human voice scores of miles.

The year after his birth the first steamship crossed the Atlantic. Now every ocean is stirred by the swift messengers of nations in peace and war. The world of mind and morals has been evolving new theories of thought and new rules of social and spiritual life. The activity of human genius has brought out new creations in every department of utility. Ancient institutions have given place to new and more refined and delicate ones.

The wonders of art have outstripped the wildest visions of dreaming fancy and given to human achievement boundless possibilities, that may cover the earth with charities and blessings that will wipe away all tears and lull into sweet harmony the sighs and sorrows of the human race.

Amid this wonderful impulse of human action this distinguished man has lived and acted and enrolled his name.

Mr. President, when the end came to those eighty years of arduous life, when the golden bowl was broken, and the silver cord was loosed, and the pitcher broken at the fountain, it could be truthfully said of my colleague that "he died at his post." If not like Chatham falling on the floor of the House of Lords, or John Quincy Adams sinking in the House of Representatives, yet he succumbed from the exertion and the labor of his Senatorial duties like the great English leader and the exalted American ex-President.

The unswerving patriot, ISHAM G. HARRIS, whose long life had been devoted to his country, had striven to the end, and his last days were his best days.

He is now in his grave

> After life's fitful fever he sleeps well.

Neither the call to the hustings, the concourse of admiring friends, the contests in the Senate, nor "the rapture of the fight" shall again summon him to duty. His repose is tranquil in the sacred precincts of Elmwood, overlooking in its beauty and silence the Mississippi as it swells in majestic flow at the base of Memphis, the beautiful city of the valley. Peace to his ashes.

ADDRESS OF MR. MORRILL.

Mr. MORRILL. Mr. President, generally members of the Senate when first elected are no longer young, and their early departure to "the silent land" is in accordance with nature. Within the past year the decease of Senators and ex-Senators has been unprecedented. The list of ex-Senators includes twelve—Voorhees, McPherson, Doolittle, Cameron, Dolph, McMillan, Coke, Dixon, Jones, Robinson, Clingman, and Paddock; and the seats here of three Senators were also made vacant, or those so recently occupied by Earle and George and by Senator HARRIS, of Tennessee, to whose memory the Senate to-day offers its tribute of respect.

All of these men possessed some characteristic and prominent merits which were appreciated by their people at home, as well as by their associates here, who knew them at close range. McPherson, Voorhees, and HARRIS were all recent members of the Committee on Finance, and whatever differences on political and economical questions may have existed, the committee, I feel authorized to say, were personally all friends, and the survivors are here to-day as mourners.

Our late and long-time associate, Senator HARRIS, of Tennessee, was born in the State he represented, where, as it may safely be assumed, his political influence was probably never surpassed, except by that of General Jackson, whose wide national renown served to gild and expand his local influence at home. Nearly fifty years ago ISHAM G. HARRIS served in the Thirtieth and Thirty-first Congress as a member of the House of Representatives, then for six years as governor of Tennessee, and during the last three years of the rebellion he was a volunteer aid of the "Confederate Army of Tennessee," as he preferred to state it himself in the Congressional Directory. It may be inferred that as a stanch partisan of the State-rights doctrine and a veteran supporter of the Virginia resolutions of 1798 he rather preferred to be a volunteer aid to the Confederate Army of Tennessee than of the army under the direct control of Jefferson Davis.

Not obtrusively aspiring to be a national leader, yet he was a leader, and often consulted by his friends and his party. While always courageously stiff in his opinions, these were usually found to be safely behind the political breastworks of the Democratic party.

Tennessee was the home of Senator HARRIS and also of John Bell, who in 1860 received the vote of Tennessee for the Presidency as the candidate of the so-called "South American" or Union party; but Tennessee would hardly have been induced to join the Southern Confederacy in 1861 solely because of the Republican election of Mr. Lincoln to the Presidency but for the potential influence of Governor HARRIS.

Near the close of the rebellion, having been a Confederate with many conspicuous proofs, he deemed it wise to leave the country, lest the exigencies of peace might prove more portentous than those of war, and at once departed for Mexico, taking with him for safe-keeping—whatever Parson Brownlow may then have erroneously supposed—$60,000 belonging to the State, but which was safely brought back by him and returned to the State treasury.

After a brief sojourn in Mexico, he went to Great Britain, and there finally concluded, after all his recent experience, there was no place so dear to him as his old home in Tennessee, and to that he returned in 1867.

In 1877 Mr. HARRIS was elected to the United States Senate, where he was for twenty years a very prominent and useful member. As the chairman of the Committee on the District of Columbia, its various duties were discharged with ability and with nearly universal approval. He was long a valuable member of the Senate Committee on Finance, always in attendance at every meeting of the committee promptly on time, and bills submitted to him for examination and report were sure of early attention. He rarely made what are called prepared or set speeches; but, as long as health permitted, when the Senate was in session, he was here in daily attendance.

Senator HARRIS was a radical adherent to his party, and when he felt it as his sacred duty to denounce the measures of his political opponents, it was apparent from the unction of his accentuation and his dramatic gesticulation that he was ready to strike, if not with the sword of the Lord, certainly with nothing less than the sword of Gideon.

Early becoming familiar with the parliamentary rules of the Senate, Senator HARRIS, as the President pro tempore or when invited to the chair by the presiding officer, discharged its duties not only with excellent ability and absolute impartiality, but with extreme brevity.

Socially he was not egotistical, and never by his conversation made a darling of himself. Even his age was long kept as a personal secret about which the public had no business to inquire.

For many years, in my absence, Senator HARRIS was my standing pair, and it was very scrupulously observed.

He was a frank, outspoken man, and did not hide his opinions by silence or by a forky tongue. His integrity appeared to me absolute and unimpeachable. Here he was respected as well as esteemed—certainly he was esteemed by me—and had I preceded him—

> To the undiscovered country from whose bourne
> No traveler returns—

as perhaps from seniority of age might have been expected. I do not doubt he would have tendered a just and kind word in my behalf. But it was long ago written, "There shall be two men in the field ; one shall be taken and one is left."

ADDRESS OF MR. MORGAN.

Mr. MORGAN. Mr. President, I first saw ISHAM G. HAR-RIS near Nashville, in Tennessee, when he was governor of that State and had been driven from his capital by the Federal Army under General Buell. He came to the head of a column I was leading in a reconnoissance under the orders of General Forrest.

He came as an aid-de-camp of that distinguished officer, bearing orders for my execution.

In that brief interview I saw a characteristic display of the intrepidity of the man.

The action was perilous and the governor went into the fight with the dash and resolution that plainly revealed his character as a soldier who rejoiced on the field of battle.

This gallant soldier passed out of my observation into the high career of splendid service in which he won great distinction as the honored adviser of the eminent men who led the destiny of the Confederacy. No true soldier ever failed to recognize in him a brother in arms, and a brother in every emergency.

When that war had ended, the people of Tennessee conferred on him the highest honor in their gift by choosing him as a Senator of the United States. It was my fortune to meet Mr. HARRIS the second time on the floor of the Senate, as a Senator from Alabama, on March 4, 1877, and we took up the grave duties of that office on the same day, he representing my native State.

I had not seen him since the morning of our brief association on the field of battle.

S. Doc. 343——3

Henceforth our efforts were to be devoted to the service of the country in fields where peace harvests "her victories more renowned than war."

It is a cause for deep pride to me that in the twenty years of our service in the Senate we never differed on any great leading question of public policy that involved a question of the proper construction of the Constitution of the United States, for he was a true and wise man, whose matured opinions were carefully formed and were always presented with the emphasis of profound conviction and maintained with unflinching courage.

No name in the annals of the South is more honored in the esteem of the people than that of ISHAM G. HARRIS as a statesman and wise legislator. His fidelity to every public trust became a standard in the minds of the people for the highest duty of an American Senator, and in the Senate that standard is recognized as being worthy of the best men of the best days of the Republic.

The history of this noble and genuine man can not be stated in a single address, nor, indeed, in any single statement of tongue or pen. There are treasured in the hearts of millions of people the legends of ISHAM G. HARRIS, that are kept fresh and green by the pulsations of gratitude. These are often repeated at the fireside and to listening groups of children as proofs of the qualities that they should prefer to all other attributes or accomplishments.

His life grew to full development in an atmosphere of immaculate honor until it became a noble structure to stand for all time as a high model of the typical Southern man. I feel intense pride in the privilege of referring to ISHAM G. HARRIS in this splendid attitude in which he is placed by the universal opinion of the Southern people. It is descriptive of their sentiments on all great questions and of their manner of dealing with matters of public concern with honest directness of purpose and action.

It is well for us and for our successors in the Senate that we have his record as a guide to correct and just action in the great questions that we must deal with in this great Forum.

In this hour of suspense and anxiety that clothes the whole body of the people with a deep spirit of inquiry as to our duty to the honor of the Republic and a deeper resolve to protect and defend it to the uttermost, it would give me the most sincere satisfaction if we could invoke the advantage of his wisdom and his true and courageous sense of duty to advise the Senate as to its course, now pressing for determination.

His counsels would not be rash, but they would be just and courageous, and his advocacy of a righteous line of action would give to our resolution the confidence of worthy motives and assured success in a new and delicate line of duty to which we are impelled by the claims of humanity upon the heart of the great and magnanimous American people.

I can pronounce no higher eulogium upon the character of this great Senator than to voice the wish of the Senate, if it could be so, that he could now be with us to advise us with his counsels.

It is in such moments that we miss great leaders and learn to value their worth to the country. No question was too high or too broad for the grasp of his intellect, and no matter engaged the attention of the Senate to which he refused to give his attention.

ADDRESS OF MR. HOAR.

Mr. HOAR. Mr. President, the great career of Senator HAR
RIS is well known to his countrymen. He has been for more
than a generation a striking and conspicuous figure in our
public life. His colleague, his successor, the men of his own
political faith, the people of the great State which he served
and honored and loved so long, will, each in their own way,
portray his character and record their esteem and affection.

My tribute must be that of a political opponent. So far as I
have been able to exert any influence upon the history of my
country during the long conflict now happily past, it has been
in opposition to him, to the party to which he belonged, to the
opinions which he held, I am sure, quite as zealously and conscientiously as I hold my own.

We entered the Senate on the same day. He was a Southerner, a Democrat, and a Confederate. I was born and bred in
New England, a Republican, and an Abolitionist. We rarely
spoke in the same debate except on different sides. Yet I have
no memory of him that is not tender and affectionate, and there
is nothing that I can honestly say of him except words of
respect and of honor.

He was a typical Southerner. He had the virtues and the
foibles that belonged to that character in the generation the last
of whom are now passing from the stage of public action. He
was a man of very simple and very high qualities; he was a
man of absolute frankness in public behavior and in private
dealing. The thought that was in his heart corresponded absolutely with the utterance of his lips. He had nothing to conceal. I was about to say he was a man without the gift of

diplomacy; but he was a man with the gift of the highest diplomacy—directness, simplicity, frankness, courage—qualities which make always their way to their mark and to their goal over all circumlocutions and ambiguities.

He was a man of brief, clear, and compact speech. He would sum up in a few vigorous and ringing sentences the argument to which other men would give hours or days. He had an instinct for the hinge or turning point of a debate.

He was a man of absolute integrity and steadfastness. What he said, that he would do. Where you left him, there, so long as he lived, you would find him when you came back. He was a man of unflinching courage. He was not afraid of any antagonist, whether in the hall of debate or on the field of battle.

He was an acknowledged master of parliamentary law, a system upon which not only the convenient procedure of legislative bodies largely depends, but which has close relations to constitutional liberty itself. How often a few simple and clear sentences of his have dispersed the clouds and brought order out of confusion in this Chamber.

His great legislative experience made him invaluable as a servant of his own State, of the country, and as a councilor to his younger associates.

He was a pleasant man in private intercourse. He had great sense of humor, a gift of portraiture, a good memory. So he brought out of the treasure-house of his varied experience abundant matter for the delight of young and old. There is no man left in the Senate who was better company in hours of recreation.

His influence will be felt here for a long time. His striking figure will still seem to be hovering about the Senate Chamber, still sitting, still deliberating, still debating.

Mr. President, it is delightful to think how, during the lives of the men who took part in the great conflict which preceded and followed the civil war and the greater conflict of the war itself, the old bitterness and estrangements are all gone. Throughout the whole land the word "countryman" has at last become a title of endearment. The memory of the leaders of that great conflict is preserved as tenderly by the men who fought with them as by the men who followed them. Massachusetts joins with Tennessee in laying a wreath on the tomb of her great soldier, her great governor, her great Senator. He was faithful to truth as he saw it; to duty as he understood it; to constitutional liberty as he conceived it.

If, as some of us think, he erred, his error was that of a brave man ready to give life and health and hope to the unequal struggle.

> To his loved cause he offered, free from stain,
> Courage and faith; vain faith and courage vain.

And, Mr. President, when he returned to his allegiance, he offered to the service of his reunited country the same zeal and devotion he had given to the Confederacy. There was no reserved or half-hearted loyalty. We could have counted on his care for the honor and glory of the country, on his wise and brave counsel, in this hour of anxiety with an unquestioning confidence. So Massachusetts to-day presses the hand of Tennessee and mourns with her for her great citizen who has departed.

ADDRESS OF MR. WALTHALL.

Mr. WALTHALL.. Mr. President, when the people of a Congressional district, after a public servant has been tried and tested in other positions of responsibility, elect him two terms to Congress and offer him a third, it is but a just recognition of his fidelity and usefulness by the beneficiaries of his service.

When later the people of his State, with the record of his public service before them, elect him their governor three times in succession, these added honors attest their appreciation of his growing capacities and prove his increased popularity and influence.

When the representatives of the same people, voicing their will, after a great war had intervened and their favorite citizen had rendered three years of military service in a conspicuous position, at a trying time summon him from private life to accept the highest trust his State has the power to bestow, electing him four times consecutively, twice after he had passed the age of 70, to the Senate of the United States, then all has been done that the people of a single State can do to honor and glorify a public servant, whatever his merit and ability.

And when the same people who had thus honored him in life lament his death as a personal bereavement and a great public misfortune alike; when the State clothes herself in mourning and throughout all her borders the population, in vast assemblies, in church and court room and in the market place, everywhere, in public and in private, manifest their devotion and their grief; when Congressmen in both Houses and officials in all departments of the Government bear witness to his worth; when from no quarter of the Union comes a harsh word of criticism upon any feature of his eventful career—when we have seen all this, we feel that what came after death was but a natural sequence and fit complement to all that went before; but we wonder that a long career of active, positive, forceful, uncompromising leadership should be followed by such universal tributes of approval and respect. Yet these honors and these tributes were bestowed upon the late Senator HARRIS, living and dead, and how well they all were earned is known of all men familiar with the history of his life, which has been so admirably outlined to-day by the senior Senator from Tennessee, for many years his coworker and associate.

For a young man of limited means and with but a slender educational groundwork to fit himself for the practice of a learned profession in the intervals of the employment by which he earns his living is but the story of many a brave-hearted American's early life. But when such a man makes his way from the starting point of a country merchant's store through other places of distinction up to the Senate of the United States and promptly becomes an acknowledged power here, and for twenty years holds high rank among the foremost members of the body, we must look elsewhere than to mere diligence and positive capacity, or to scheming, or to some accident or freak of fortune which sometimes thrusts mediocrity into temporary prominence, in searching for the secret of such remarkable success.

From causes like these men without aptitude or merit may occupy high places for a time, but without proven fitness for usefulness in some form, turned practically to some valuable account in which the public is directly concerned, a public man's hold upon the confidence of his own people and that of his associates in service can never long endure. When it lasts, as the late Senator HARRIS's did, through a half century, marked by stirring and trying events and the shifting fortunes of other men, and as time advanced grew firmer and stronger, the secret must be found in some of those rare attributes which in such combination and degree are denied to men in general.

After cordial personal intercourse and intimate party association with him for many years, through which I closely observed his dealings with both men and measures, my belief is that force and faith were the powers which chiefly contributed to his achievements in life.

Force of intellect, supported by the force of a vigorous physical organism equal to any strain, mapped out his plans and purposes with steadiness and continuity; the force of a clear, sententious, and incisive style of argument urged them and impressed them, and force of character, will power that would not be thwarted and could not be subdued, impelled them with persistency and power to consummation and conclusion.

Faith in himself, in his own power and purity of motive, gave him strength and independence and made him aggressive, persistent, and well-nigh irresistible in the pursuit of all his purposes. He had faith in our form of government, in the permanence of our institutions, in the masses of the people, and in their capacity to govern themselves; faith in his own construction of the Federal Constitution, from which he never swerved, and in his own ideals, which were exalted, of justice and duty, of manliness and honor.

He was faithful to principle and to every trust, however great or small; to State, constituents, and friends, and to every obligation they imposed upon him. Stern, direct, incorruptible, and resolute, he encountered enmities and was sometimes a mark for slander; but the charge was never made that he failed to keep faith with any one of his fellow-men.

If, as I believe, the faculties and sentiments I have attributed to our late associate belonged to him, we need search no further for the secret of his successes and his long career of usefulness and honor, for the results were no more than the causes deserved. If they did not, I have misconceived his character, although, with excellent opportunities, I have studied his life with interest and have much reason to lament his death sincerely.

ADDRESS OF MR. HAWLEY.

Mr. HAWLEY. Mr. President, the full and interesting sketches of Senator HARRIS's life and character to which we have listened leave me little to say beyond testifying my personal regard for him. I congratulate myself that what I had previously intended to say coincides so well with the observations of the Senator from Massachusetts [Mr. Hoar].

Mr. HARRIS was a man of strong convictions—frank and brave in setting forth and defending them. He was always ready for combat, prompt in repartee, skillful in attack and defense. He sometimes struck heavily, but never with personal malice, and no man remembers him unkindly. He was a master of parliamentary law, and in his frequent occupancy of the chair he knew well how to keep the true question before the Senate and how to preserve order.

He was a gallant and chivalrous man, a foremost champion of what he desired to promote. His bearing is well remembered, but can not be described. He differed at one time from many of us on great issues, but none doubted his sincerity and courage.

In private life he was a cordial, genial, hospitable, and typical gentleman of whatever school.

Tennessee honors herself in honoring his memory. The Senate records its affection and respect, and will not forget him.

ADDRESS OF MR. COCKRELL.

Mr. COCKRELL. Mr. President, ISHAM GREEN HARRIS, to whose imperishable memory the Senate of the United States pays this last memorial tribute, was born in Franklin County, Tenn., on the 10th day of February, 1818, being the youngest of five sons and four daughters born to Isham Harris and his wife, Lucy Davidson Harris, and died in this city on the 8th day of July, 1897, in the eightieth year of his age.

He was endowed with a strong, vigorous constitution and a clear, active, quickly grasping intellect, and was reared amid rural scenes and healthful surroundings.

His education was limited, and only such as a newly settled country afforded. He attended Winchester Academy, and at the early age of 14 years his untiring energy, indomitable will, independence, and self-reliance carried him away from home to engage in the active affairs of life.

He went to Paris, Tenn., and began his eventful career as a clerk in a mercantile establishment, and by his energy, intelligent devotion to his duties, and strict economy was in a few years enabled to engage in business on his own account in Ripley, Miss., and proved a successful merchant.

This avocation was not the goal of his aspirations and laudable ambition. While successfully conducting his mercantile business he was studying law at night and preparing for a broader field of action. Having accumulated sufficient means to enable him for a time to devote his whole time to the study of his chosen profession, he returned to Paris, Tenn., in 1841 and began the practice of his profession in the office of an elder brother, an able and learned jurist. He applied himself to the study and practice of the law with his characteristic zeal, industrious application and devotion, and quickly acquired a lucrative practice and professional reputation which attracted public notice seldom attained so early in life in his profession.

In 1846 he was elected as a Democrat from his senatorial district to the general assembly of his State, and declined a reelection.

In 1848 he was chosen a candidate for Presidential elector in his Congressional district, and in the canvass displayed an ability for popular debate which secured for him the respect, admiration, and confidence of the people, which were never betrayed nor shaken in all the long years of his public career.

In 1849 he was nominated by a Democratic convention as a candidate to represent his Congressional district in Congress, and was elected by a majority greater than that of his party.

In 1851 he was renominated and reelected, and in 1853 was renominated, but declined to accept.

He then removed to Memphis, Tenn., and resumed the practice of law, and at once took rank with the leading lawyers and secured a lucrative share of the legal business.

In 1856 he was Presidential elector for the State at large on the Democratic ticket. His competitor in this canvass was the distinguished Whig, ex-Governor Neil S. Brown, a worthy foeman in public debate. In 1857 he was nominated and elected governor of his State; was reelected in 1859, and again in 1861.

His position in public affairs was never equivocal. As governor of the State and commander in chief of her military forces from 1861 to the close of the war, he did all that was in his power to secure the success of the Confederacy by organizing his State troops, going with them into camp and battle, and remained with the army to the close of the war, and served on the staff of the successive generals commanding the army of Tennessee. He was at his post of duty and danger through heat and cold rain and sunshine, in camp and on battlefield, in advance and retreat, in victory and defeat.

When the war closed, on account of the surviving passions and fierce prejudices aroused by the severe conflicts in Tennessee, he went to Mexico and remained there for eighteen months; and then went to Liverpool, England, and engaged successfully in mercantile business for one year, and then returned to Memphis and resumed the practice of law, and closely applied himself for ten years.

In 1877 he was elected a Senator from the State of Tennessee in the Senate of the United States; was reelected in 1883 and in 1889, and in 1895 for the term ending March 3, 1901.

By this brief sketch of his illustrious life we may profit, as well as the young men of this and coming generations of our great country, to whom we present him as an example, not to deter, but to follow. From his fourteenth year of age to his eightieth – sixty-six years – he was in active life; not a drone, but emphatically a busy bee, neither losing nor wasting time.

In whatever avocation or position he engaged or accepted, he was preeminently successful and useful. To the discharge of all the duties and obligations of his avocation or position, however humble or exalted, he devoted his whole time, energy, attention, and abilities closely, industriously, and intelligently.

He was truly the "architect of his own fortune." His example proves that success can be achieved by great labor, and that life gives nothing worthy of a noble manhood without such labor. As a State senator in the general assembly of his native State he was laborious, useful, and ranked among its ablest members, and acquitted himself to the entire satisfaction of his constituency, and was tendered and declined a renomination. As a Representative in the Congress of the United States, although one of its youngest members, he quickly won a high position as a practical legislator, a sound lawyer, and an able debater, and so acceptably to his constituency discharged the duties that he was renominated and elected and tendered a third nomination, which he declined.

He was three times nominated and elected governor of his State, which fact attests his fidelity and efficiency. As a Senator, for punctuality and promptness in his attendance upon the sessions of the Senate and the meetings of the many committees of which he was a member he had few equals and no superiors. From his entrance to the close of his life he was continuously a member of the District of Columbia Committee and chairman when his party was in control. He was a member of the Committee on Finance during the Forty-ninth to the Fifty-fifth Congress, and served during the Forty-fifth and Forty-sixth Congresses on the Committee on Claims, and was most useful and laborious.

He served as a member of the Committee on Rules during the Forty-eighth to the Fifty-fifth Congress. He was a member of many other committees and gave close attention to his duties on each.

When his party was in control he was unanimously chosen President pro tempore. As a parliamentarian he had no superior in the Senate, and presided with dignity, marked courtesy, and unquestioned impartiality.

Of the 76 members of the Senate when he entered upon his duties on March 4, 1877, the Forty-fifth Congress, only 6 Senators are now members.

During his entire service in this Chamber it was my privilege to be on terms of the closest intimacy and warmest friendship with him. I respected, honored, and loved him for his nobleness of character, his sound judgment, his wise and judicious counsel, and his unquestionable integrity.

Without any disparagement or reflection upon the valuable services of any other members of this Senate, during his long service here I can frankly and truthfully say that in my judgment he had no superior in discharging the varied duties, responsibilities, and obligation devolving upon Senators.

Few men in public life have had intrusted to them the duties and reponsibilities, the trusts and the honors assigned to him by the good people of his State. At all times and under all circumstances he fully met the expectations of his constituents, and to the last enjoyed their respect, confidence, and admiration.

In this Chamber we have lost an able, earnest, efficient, incorruptible, and wise Senator. Full of years, full of honors, he has gone, to return no more, leaving to his family, his State, and his country a character, a record, an example worthy of the emulation of all.

ADDRESS OF MR. STEWART.

Mr. STEWART. Mr. President, the character and career of Senator HARRIS inspire the strongest faith that can possibly be afforded in the perpetuity of our institutions. Rising, as he did, from the ranks of the people by his own unaided exertions, and accomplishing the great results which he did during a long and eventful life, he presents to all young men the great possibilities for advancement which exist in this free country. In no other country on this globe and in no other age could such a career be possible.

When we behold the great and good men which this country has produced and continues to produce, when we find men on all occasions equal to the great emergencies which are presented, no matter how overwhelming they may appear, we feel more and more confidence in the future of our country, for we know that these examples will inspire those who come after us as the examples of the great men who have preceded us have inspired this generation.

Senator HARRIS was a remarkable man. He had a grasp of intellect which condensed volumes into sentences. He had a fidelity to truth which never allowed him to swerve or go back from it. He remained throughout his long and illustrious life in touch with the people amongst whom he had lived and with whom he had always the warmest sympathy. It was manifest to those who associated with him that in all he did his inspiration was a desire to benefit and serve the people of the United States.

It is not strange that such a sentiment on his part was appreciated by the people of his State and all who had the honor of knowing him. That, sir, was the secret of the confidence which

S. Doc. 343——4

was reposed in him. His confidence in and his reliance on the people inspired them with confidence in return, and so they trusted and honored him. He has furnished an example which gladdens the hearts of all who love their country and who desire to improve the condition of the people.

ADDRESS OF MR. CHILTON.

Mr. CHILTON. Mr. President, while I did not know Senator HARRIS with the intimacy of long personal association, I have since a boy been familiar with his writings, speeches, and public conduct.

The State in which I live has been supplied abundantly from the great State of Tennessee. Many of our best citizens emigrated to Texas from that Commonwealth; and I have noticed that they all seem to know and to love ISHAM G. HARRIS.

So when I first came to the Senate for a short term by appointment of the governor, more than six years ago, I felt that curiosity about Senator HARRIS which always animates younger men to know the actors in great events, sharpened by the recollection of stories told concerning his achievements by those who had long been his personal friends.

When I first saw him, in 1891, he was well-ripened and probably at his best.

I have often watched him, in the cloak room, in his Senatorial seat, in the chair of the presiding officer, and he always seemed the same. I do not remember ever to have heard him laugh aloud. There was the twinkle in the eye, the manifest enjoyment in the general merriment, but he never appeared to "turn himself loose."

I picture him as he would come into the Senate Chamber. There, in his familiar place on the right of the Vice-President, in the front row, he would take his seat. He hardly seems to say anything, as if by previous design. He seems never to make an occasion, but to find it in the current proceedings as set on foot by others. He seems to spy out that something is taking an irregular direction and that he must set it right.

He first asks a question or calls for the reading of some document, as if he imperfectly understood it. Then he proceeds to clear up all doubts. First emphasis, then gesticulation—no, not in succession, but an indescribable combination of emphasis and gesticulation.

Attention has often been called to his absolute primacy in the Senate on all questions relating to parliamentary law. Up to the very hour of his last appearance here he was so clear and so magisterial that he never lost his authority in that field.

As has been stated, his service in Congress began in the House of Representatives at the session which convened in December, 1849, and in that, his first session of service, he exhibited that peculiar interest in questions of legislative practice which marked his long Senatorial career, for the reporter makes the following observation touching the proceedings of a particular day.

Some conversation followed on points of order, in which Messrs. HARRIS of Tennessee, White, Disney, Rumsey, Wentworth, and the Speaker participated.

During his four years in the House I find that he made only one set speech. The Wilmot proviso, with all its exciting incidents, was then the subject of consideration. In that speech we find the same principles, the same habits of thought and manner which marked his life fifty years afterwards. There was brevity, for though the contest was prolonged and the temptation to digress great, he spoke but an hour. There was the strict construction of the Constitution, for he dwelt on the rule that Congress possesses no powers except those expressly delegated by the Constitution or necessary to the exercise of some expressly delegated power; and he, who rarely ever quoted, repeats in that speech the words of another great American in protest against those "vagrant, wandering powers that find no congenial spot on which to rest upon the broad face of the Constitution of the country.''

This was his chart of political action in every place of duty. He followed it after leaving Congress in 1853, and it governed his action during all those stirring years which led up to the civil war.

Perhaps the most eventful part of the life of Senator HARRIS was that which related to the great organization of secession. The governors of the Southern States in 1861 were almost without exception men of strong character and ability. Perhaps the most remarkable of these governors were Brown of Georgia, Letcher of Virginia, Sam Houston of Texas, and HARRIS of Tennessee.

In the difficulties of their surroundings and in vigor of intellectual comprehension, the Texas and Tennessee governors stand highest among this group.

Sam Houston was a strong Union man. The whole secession movement was resolutely combated by him, but, notwithstanding his extraordinary power in Texas, he found himself gradually submerged by a rising wave of public sentiment which finally reached the velocity of a torrent, drove him out of the governor's chair, and took the State out of the Union. There was the spectacle of a man who had been strong in the affections of his State overridden by an excited and determined people, and unable, with all his popularity and influence, to make the slightest headway. He stood almost alone, a Unionist and a conservative, in the midst of organized, indignant, irreconcilable revolution.

The situation of Governor HARRIS in Tennessee was quite a different one. He sympathized with secession, he wanted to take his State out of the Union, and he used his powers and his influence to accomplish the very result which Sam Houston had endeavored to obstruct in Texas. His task was not like that which fell to the hands of the governors in States like South Carolina, Alabama, Mississippi, and Louisiana, where both the people and the executive, with common impulse, hailed the banner of a new confederation. On the contrary, a powerful section of the Tennessee people, led by Andrew Johnson, a great Senator belonging to the same party, confronted Governor HARRIS in his policy of secession.

We need not dwell upon the details of that struggle, but it is enough to say that the courage, tenacity, and generalship of HARRIS prevailed against the combined efforts of Whig and Democratic Union leaders in Tennessee and added that State to the number of those which constituted the Southern Confederacy.

ISHAM G. HARRIS was one of the few public men of whom the people never seemed to tire.

Ordinarily popularity is fleeting. The remarkable changes which come over the House and the Senate in the course of a single decade attest the instability of official tenure; but a few men seem proof against all disfavor; if they are ever criticized their critics are forgotten; if condemned for a vote they are forgiven. To carry opposition to the point of actually defeating their reelection would be considered at home a sort of high treason. So strong is the general confidence in their high purpose and right judgment that it always prevails over minor difficulties when election day rolls around.

Senator HARRIS was one of these rare characters. He was the hero not only of Tennessee but of Tennesseans scattered throughout the Union. He grew, in their estimation, to be a sort of lineal successor to Andrew Jackson. His name and life and peculiarities always touched their enthusiasm.

Perhaps the most impressive thing in his strong individuality

was his willingness always to take responsibility and his absolute unconcern about results—that cheerful faith that the right
will take care of itself and that there need be no anxiety on the
part of a public man except the anxiety to be right.

I have seen men whom God had blessed with conscience and
courage, but not with equanimity, so that, knowing the truth
and voting the truth, they were still nervous that they should
not be misunderstood and fidgeting about consequences which
they were determined to face.

Not so with Senator HARRIS. He seemed to think that a
man who acted truly upon his convictions of right held an absolute insurance policy against all disaster at the hands of the
people.

What a great life may be worked out on that sort of logic.
You may put a small man in Congress, and if he looks at every
question as it arises with a heart single and an eye single to
finding out the right, in a few years such a dignity will be
given to his apparent mediocrity that he will gradually emerge
above the level of his fellows and assume a consideration in the
country which will make men wonder at the secret of his rise.

If men of moderate mind can be thus lifted by the practice of
simple straightforwardness, how splendid becomes the principle
when it acts on a man of native intellectual power and force of
character? This was the combination in the case of ISHAM G.
HARRIS. He was always clear, always firm, always true,
always great.

Mr. TURLEY. Mr. President, for more than fifty years the name of ISHAM G. HARRIS has been a household word and a tower of strength in the State of Tennessee. Probably no other man in the history of the State has exercised so potent an influence upon its fortunes and its destiny. Once he served it in the legislature twice as Presidential elector, twice in the House of Representatives, three times as governor, for four years in war, and four times in the Senate of the United States. Every honor that the people of Tennessee could confer was bestowed on him. Other of her sons may have served her longer in particular departments, but no other one has served her in so many ways or so long and so faithfully as he did.

His power and influence in his native State may be illustrated by the political change brought about by him in 1856. From 1832, the year in which Andrew Jackson was elected to his second term, to 1856, when James Buchanan was the Democratic candidate—a period of twenty-four years—the State of Tennessee had been a Whig stronghold. In 1856 ISHAM G. HARRIS was an elector at large on the Buchanan ticket. The Whigs elected ex-Governor Neil S. Brown to uphold the principles of their party. The canvass made by those great sons of Tennessee is historic in our State. In the judgment of a people who had been accustomed to listen to such men as Grundy, Gentry, Andrew Johnson, Cave Johnson, Polk, Jones, and others of that class, it was pronounced the most remarkable and profound discussion of great political questions which had ever occurred in the State, and all felt that for years it would settle and control the political character and policy of Tennessee.

Governor Brown was a man of great intellect and matchless

powers of oratory. He was a man of winning and popular manners; and he had behind him a compact, powerful party, flushed with a quarter of a century of continuous victory. But nothing could resist the earnestness, the force and power of ISHAM G. HARRIS. The campaign was a death blow to the Whig party, and from that time forth Tennessee has been a Democratic State.

Senator HARRIS was one of those rare men who seemed fitted physically, mentally, and morally for every phase and condition, every changing emergency of life.

His appearance was pleasing and impressive. Above the middle height, his figure was well proportioned and compact. His eyes were piercing and full of intelligence. His features were strong and framed to express and portray every feeling and sentiment of his mind and soul. With an iron constitution, which defied fatigue and disease, he possessed a vitality which seemed inexhaustible.

No one faculty of his mind was unduly developed, but each was fitted for its special functions, and all went to make up a well-rounded, perfect intellect. While he was a man of action rather than of books, yet his information was varied and accurate. He never entered upon the examination of any subject without exhausting all the means of information at his command. Men and affairs he studied well and accurately.

He was both passionate and impulsive; but his impulses were high and honorable, and his fiery passions were controlled by his indomitable will and his strict sense of justice. He was fluent and brilliant in conversation; courteous and gallant in bearing and demeanor. Possessed of an undaunted courage that knew not fear, he had at the same time as kind and sympathetic a heart as ever beat in human bosom. His life was one long series of kind deeds and concealed charities. He was the genius of forceful action, of industry and work. He never tired

Of his rugged honesty and his unspotted honor I need not speak. They are known of all men. He was ambitious of fame, character, distinction, and achievements; and, while he was aggressive and impatient of opposition, yet no man was ever more thoughtful and considerate of the rights and feelings of others.

There have been greater orators than ISHAM G. HARRIS, but few greater debaters; men more learned in books and theories, but few better versed in all the practical affairs of life. There have been lawyers more distinguished, statesmen more renowned, men better equipped in special fields and for particular work, but it is hard to conceive, take him all in all, of a more forceful and efficient man, a man better qualified to impress himself upon his life and times, than was ISHAM G. HARRIS.

We can see this from his long, adventurous, and remarkable career. A penniless youth, he became a successful merchant before he was 21; a lawyer of prominence and distinction before he was 25; a member of the legislature before he was 30; a member of the House of Representatives at 31; governor of his State at 39; an exile from his country at 47; reduced again to poverty before he was 50, he became once more a merchant, and then a lawyer, and finally a Senator in the Congress of the United States—equally great, forceful, and self-reliant under all these conditions and in all these places and positions.

The universality, if I may so call it, of his character and mind especially marked him as a lawyer. He was equally strong and vigorous in every branch of his profession. His practice embraced all the courts. Those who were thrown with him could scarcely tell when he appeared at his best. Sometimes it seemed in the heat and fire of a great criminal trial, when the life of a client hung on the issue, and again when he was bringing the strength of his intellect to the elucidation of some intricate principle before a learned chancellor or the highest tribunal of his State.

No lawyer in Tennessee ever had greater power and influence on its courts and juries, and I may add here that no client who had a just cause was ever turned away by him because he was unable to bring with him a fee. His services were always open to the poor and distressed without fee and without price.

He could and would go to any just length in behalf of what he believed to be right, but at the same time he was practical and conservative. This latter phase of his character is shown by his conduct after his return to Tennessee from his exile in Mexico and England. The South was in the throes of the reconstruction period; negro suffrage had just been established; passion ran riot; and the feeling of hostility against the General Government was, if possible, more intense than during the time of flagrant war. All eyes were at once turned toward him. By his example, by his conduct, and by his advice he counseled moderation and a dignified acquiescence in the new order of things—the inevitable. And no man in Tennessee or in the South did more to bring about that era of good feeling which now exists between the two sections and to revive in the Southern heart that sense of loyalty to and patriotism for our common country which had been stifled by the fierce strife of civil war.

His fairness, his justice, his frank, outspoken, upright character are evidenced by the strong hold he always had on his political opponents. In his hottest political battles he commanded the respect, the esteem, the admiration of those with whom he contended.

His long career in this body is a part of the history of our country. Of his services here others are better qualified to speak than am I.

I can not recall the time when I did not know him. His older sons were my schoolmates and friends. I was raised to respect him as the greatest of living Tennesseans. From my earliest manhood up to the time of his death our relations were most intimate and confidential. I can say of him what Judge Haywood, the early historian of our State, said of Gen. James Robertson, one of its noblest pioneers:

He was a man who by his actions merited all the eulogium, esteem, and affection which the most ardent of his countrymen have ever bestowed upon him. Like almost all of those in America who have attained eminent celebrity, he had not a noble lineage to boast of nor the escutcheoned armorials of a splendid ancestry; but he had what was far more valuable, a sound mind, a healthy constitution, a robust frame, a love of virtue, an intrepid soul, and an emulous desire for honest fame.

Mr. BATE. I ask that the speech made by the Senator from Indiana [Mr. Turpie] on the occasion of the memorial at Memphis, Tenn., the home of Senator HARRIS, as a representative of the Senate, having been selected by the committee, be printed in connection with the proceedings here to-day. He made a speech, and one would know what it was from the man—a very able effort and especially an analysis of Mr. HARRIS as a Senator. It was brilliant, beautiful, logical, and all that can be said about it.

The VICE-PRESIDENT. Is there objection to the request of the Senator from Tennessee? The Chair hears none, and it is so ordered.

SPEECH OF HON. DAVID TURPIE, AT MEMPHIS, TENN.

In the midst of the dearth and dryness of mind, the mere inertia and indifference that have so much beset our age, save upon the subject as to how riches may be gotten and profits may accrue it is a goodly relief as well as a wholesome solace to recall the memory of one who chose and cherished an ideal, a standard of life more noble than this—one who devoted his labor, his attention, his time, his great abilities, with incessant diligence, with unfaltering fidelity, to the public service of the people.

ISHAM G. HARRIS, President of the Senate, for more than twenty years a member of that body, was not born in the purple. He was no favored son of wealth or fortune. The circumstances of his early years were undistinguished by any prestige of superior advantage or opportunity. His education was that of the common school and the academy. For the rest he was well taught, being self-taught. He did not disparage the learning or knowledge of the schools, but he gathered wisdom yet more abundantly. Nature had so richly endowed him for the whole course of the journey of life that he needed not to tarry long by the way for other assistance.

He was a man of manifold gifts, and so truly many sided that it would be presumption in anyone to attempt to describe him except under those aspects in which he came under his observation. In the later years of his Senatorial service he was very often engaged in the discharge of the duties of the Chair. He presided with much dignity, with equal impartiality and decision. His long experience with legislative bodies, his thorough acquaintance with the rules of the Senate, and his thoughtful study of the general principles of parliamentary law had qualified him in the most eminent manner for the position to which he had been elected by the free choice of his colleagues. It was well worth a journey to Washington to see him in the chair in a full Senate at some period of lively colloquy or exciting debate.

Order reigned first in silence save as to the member who was speaking in his place. And this condition was unbroken, undisturbed, continuous; yet as President of the Senate he seldom used the gravel. The face, the figure, the whole demeanor was such as to require and enforce respect and attention. Questions of recognition were instantly decided. Interrupting messages from the House or from the President were smoothly announced and dispatched with all due celerity and the regular course of discussion was resumed. If a knot or tangle, perchance, occurred in the day's proceedings, it was untied by an explanation from the Chair so succinct in statement, so clear in its tenor and effect, so absolutely fair and candid in its purpose, that all acquiesced therein.

Sometimes near the close of a long and tedious sitting a question of order was raised which required a review of the former proceedings of the Senate for the whole day, or perhaps longer. This review, in his terms and language, was a plain, clear narration of events in the precise order of their occurrence; no step was omitted; nothing forgotten. Every amendment and modification was noticed and the time of its offer. Even the motions that failed—the unsuccessful motion to adjourn, to refer, or to reconsider—were not overlooked. His opinion was an oral transcript of the record during every hour up to the moment when the question in argument arose. It was delivered without note or memoranda, and then followed the final ruling. Such a passage in parliamentary procedure showed beyond question the most retentive power of memory, intellectual acumen and discernment, an accurate knowledge of precedent and practice, a comprehensive grasp of the present and actual condition of affairs so much required in the Presidency of the leading parliamentary body of the world.

Now and then a new Senator, unacquainted with the rules, would take the floor with an impossible motion, one out of time, out of place, contrary to rule. Such an occasion afforded an opportunity for a study of the manner of the President worthy the closest observation. With the shadow of a smile, almost suppressed, upon his face, the Chair, having heard the motion, stated that in his opinion the same could not just then be entertained, always in such an instance giving the reasons for his action, briefly, but firmly, and accompanying the ruling with a suggestion to the honorable Senator of another way in which he might probably accomplish his purpose. This was done not after the fashion of a master toward his pupil, but rather in the tone and manner of civility with which a gentleman engaged in conversation with another upon a topic of some moment in which both were interested, would remind his friend of a circumstance which he knew quite well, but had for the moment forgotten. Yet he could administer a rebuke when reproof was necessary in the most courtly phrase and with great severity, but the occasion of this exercise of discipline must have been plain, apparent, salient. It must have been some action of the offender in violation of the ordinary rules of decorum and propriety so marked as to overcome, for the time being, the natural kindness of heart and the habitual suavity of the presiding officer. For no man ever participated in the deliberations of a legislative assembly who had a more particular regard or a more considerate deference for the rights, the opinions, the feelings, and sensibilities of others.

His excellence as a presiding officer, his studies and research in the annals of Congress and in the history of precedents in free representative assemblies, caused him for many years to be consulted as an arbiter upon these subjects. It was no uncommon thing for him to be called upon in the open Senate by Senators of either side, sometimes by the Vice-President or other occupant of the chair, to deliver from his seat an opinion in regard to some disputed question of order which was at the time pending.

When he spoke thus in response to an inquiry from his seat, there was quite a difference in his tone and conduct from that which accompanied his utterances when in the chair—a difference easily observed by one accustomed to note his manner. It was seldom expressed in words, always implied by the most courteous but constant intimation. It seemed the result or effect of the change in his position. There was in both instances the same lucid statement of the point in difference, the same temperate, careful, and thoroughly rational discussion of the diverse sides of the controversy, followed by his own conclusion and the course of argument which led him thereto. But in the chair he spoke always as one having authority, an authority derived from the Constitution, vested in him as such by the suffrages of his fellow-members.

When he spoke from his seat upon like questions, his demeanor, his language, and action were no longer those of command, but of advice, of counsel. He was now the elder brother in consultation with his peers. In every mode of implication, by the tone and rhythm of the voice, by gesture, always significant and picturesque, it was made apparent that another now occupied the chair, upon whom devolved the duty of deciding, and those who had honored him by asking his views of the case were alike responsible—answerable for the action which the Senate might take, not at all bound by any judgment of his any further than reason might show its propriety.

This delicacy of adjustment to change of position was one of the most singular characteristics of his whole course. I do not suppose that he was at all conscious of it, or that it was in any wise premeditated. It was in the nature of the man. He was one of those lofty spirits who could afford not only to recognize but to defer to his associates, having such rare and absolute toleration for the freedom of speech and opinions that he declined, in such case, to dictate to others, as he would have spurned dictation to himself.

Too much praise can hardly be given him for the sedulous care, the uninterrupted regularity, with which he performed the duties of his office and of his position as a Senator. He recognized in the most practical way the several obligations which were due from him to the country at large, to his own beloved State, to the Senate, to the committees of that body, to his colleagues in both branches of the Congress, to his very numerous correspondents in all parts of the country. He seemed to have made an allotment of his time to each of these acknowledged claimants, and with respect to an engagement concerning his official action he was of all men the most precise in terms and the most punctual in performance. This regular performance of daily duty had become with him habitual— as manifest in the last days of his active service as in the beginning.

He participated very often in the debates of the Senate, but he seldom spoke at much length, insomuch that those who heard him wished most heartily, not that he had said more—for few could say as much in less compass—but that he had spoken longer. He was very forcible in colloquy, rapid and keen in retort, very able in reply. When he addressed the Senate at greater length, upon some measure of national or general concern, he used great care both in preparation and delivery.

Fact followed fact, statement succeeded statement, argument, with the reasoning in its support, was presented in the most perfect symmetry and order. If a good style has to be defined as it has been by a high authority, "as the use of proper words in proper places," he had a style most excellent. His voice was a full tenor, clear, musical resonant; the sound of it lingered in the ear after the words had ceased. To this was added a certain demeanor of the body only partially described in the term gesture since the whole person seemed to be informed with the spirit of his utterances, and when he kindled into enthusiasm, as he sometimes did, the effect was in the highest degree impressive.

He was by nature an admirable actor, without the slightest trace of art or affectation; yet, in the ordinary course of events when he rose and addressed the Chair, although something was always said, it was more especially looked for that something was to be done. His executive force, tact, and discretion were well known and highly appreciated, so that it frequently occurred that he was designated by unanimous consent to assume the parliamentary management and conduct of the most important measures. This took place with reference to the revenue bill of 1894. After its introduction and second reading, and toward the close of the general debate, he was selected to take charge of its further progress.

The measure was at that time yet in most perilous case. It was threatened with a deluge of adverse amendments, it was encountered by the sharpest and most capable opposition, it was endangered by the cold indifference of some of those who had voted in support of it, but the Senator from Tennessee did not decline the task thus given him. He was even then well stricken in years, but he was a friend of this measure. He and many others of his side earnestly desired its passage. Under these conditions his eyes were not dim, nor was his natural force abated. Through the prolonged hours of that laborious session, day and night, whenever the Senate convened, during the repeated periods of delay, obstruction, and postponement, he was always in his seat or in his place on the floor.

If any had grown weary, he was always on the alert; if some were even inclined to slumber, he was always awake upon the watch. Those present he encouraged, the absent he chided—he chided but he sent for them. Message after message, written and verbal, with his compliments, with his regards, with assurances of his highest consideration, only they must come—the absentees must attend. It was hard to decline an invitation from Senator HARRIS. It was usually more effective than a summons from the Sergeant-at-Arms.

One of the most remarkable of his varied accomplishments was that of felicitous importunity, an importunity full of ease and elegance, not discouraged by refusal, biding time in courteous patience, not to be gotten rid of either as to the man or his subject. The eye, the touch, the tone of wistful entreaty, stirred the living, and would, were that possible, have raised the dead into action in behalf of the cause for which he pleaded. The act of 1894 could hardly have failed with such an advocate. He had announced soon after taking charge of the bill that it was possible to pass it. What was possible was accomplished. The measure became the law of the land; and this result was largely due to his parliamentary tact and judgment—his patient, persistent, unwearied assiduity.

And again, at a later period in his life, when the weight of years must have pressed still more heavily upon his power of endurance, he took upon himself, at the request of those near him, the labor and duty of organizing and uniting those inside of his own political household in favor of the policy of bimetallism—a policy which he always declared involved neither change nor innovation, but was as to our law restoration, as to silver itself restitution, and a safe return to the ancient long-tried, and well-established usage and practice of our fathers. With what success he prosecuted and completed his portion of this great design the official record of the late national convention specially discloses and we all are witnesses.

It must have seemed even to his ardent zeal in the beginning a work of mountainous difficulty and of much uncertainty in the event. It involved a correspondence under his direction and supervision with persons residing in every State and Territory and Congressional district of the United States. It required a daily comparison of part with part, a summary of very numerous details, sudden and constant resort to the best method of answer and reply, information wide and accurate, with ceaseless vigilance and circumspection to the close. Such were for many months his labors, worthy of the man and of the cause.

Those versed in modern mechanism and invention have furnished us with a phrase now become quite familiar—"applied science." Called upon to designate in the briefest terms the controlling, guiding principle of a career so greatly prolonged, so highly distinguished, we might justly name it "applied common sense" in its broadest significance and in the most active development.

Action was a necessity of his being. He was as prone to take the initiative, and to keep it, as the sparks to fly upward. Someone, now many years ago, in Washington, spoke to him once about accepting a position upon the Federal bench. "No," he said, "I desire no such position. I do not wish to be tied up like a log in a raft with nothing to do but to float or to drift at the end of a line. My boat must be in the moving current. I must feel the gale; should it come, must ride out the storm, if I have nothing left but the rudder in my hand."

This readiness to participate actively in affairs was not exercised without care or caution. He was neither rash, reckless, nor indifferent to consequences. His vision, his view of men and events, was clear. He was subject to no delusions. He sometimes failed, as men must who will act while others wait, but he was of valiant heart, strenuous will, and of that fertility in resource which either eluded or defied disaster. Failure, with him, was no finality—rather a cause and occasion for further endeavor.

His life was so crowded with action that it is not known that he had the leisure, even if he had the inclination, to have left behind him a single line of personal history or reminiscence. Moreover, he was a man of strong attachments; in friendship, earnest and sincere. How he loved Memphis, the city of his home and residence! He delighted to speak of its thrift and progress, of its harbor and landings, of its public buildings and other improvements, all of which had felt the fostering hand of his care and solicitude. How inseparably his name is connected with the magnificent transit-way of commerce and travel which, hard by, spans the broad current of the Father of Waters. Often he spoke of his State, always in the language of the warmest affection—his native State, whose great and generous constituencies had so long and so bounteously given him their support and confidence.

The faculty of almost instant adaptation of himself to circumstances of whatever exigency, his manner of molding men to his side and way, his steady advance against insurmountable obstacles, his survival of the rudest shocks of adverse fortune were as manifest throughout his whole course as they are indescribable.

Witness his departure to Mexico at the conclusion of the great civil war, his adventurous sojourn within the domain of that

Republic, his voyage to England, for he crossed the ocean not in quest of ease, but of fresh fields of new enterprise; his return to Tennessee and to this city, the reentry upon the business of his profession, his continuous and very successful practice in the courts, the canvass for his first election to the Senate, his successive reelections to that position—these are testimonials written at large to the genius, character, and conduct of one destined to so conspicuous a career.

Last scene of all—his death at the capital—at his place and post of duty, the obsequies in the Senate Chamber, the funeral cortége thence bearing his remains to their final resting place, a whole city in mourning to receive them, a State—the whole sisterhood of States—in sorrowing sympathy with you for a loss so irreparable, commemorating with you, my hearers, also to-day the demise of a great statesman whose course, with all its vicissitudes, has been in the end so grandly crowned with years, with honors, and with the just fame which follows a life so useful and beneficent.

The Vice-President. The ceremonies having been concluded, by virtue of the last of the series of resolutions heretofore adopted, the Senate stands adjourned.

The Senate accordingly (at 4 o'clock and 20 minutes p. m.) adjourned until Monday, March 28, 1898, at 12 o'clock meridian.

Proceedings in the House.

Mr. Moon. Mr. Speaker, as a mark of respect to the memory of the late Senator Harris, of Tennessee, I move that this House now suspend business until 12 o'clock to-morrow.

The motion was agreed to unanimously; and the House accordingly (at 12 o'clock and 5 minutes p. m.) took a recess until 12 o'clock to-morrow.

71

EULOGIES ON THE LATE SENATOR HARRIS

Mr. McMILLIN. Mr. Speaker, I offer the resolutions which I send to the Clerk's desk, pursuant to the special order.

The SPEAKER pro tempore. The Clerk will report the resolutions.

The resolutions were read, as follows:

Resolved, That the business of the House be now suspended that opportunity may be given for fitting tribute to the memory of Hon. ISHAM G. HARRIS, late a Senator from the State of Tennessee.

Resolved, That, as an additional mark of respect to his memory and eminent service, at the conclusion of these memorial proceedings the House stand adjourned.

Resolved, That a copy of these resolutions be transmitted by the Clerk of the House to the family of the deceased.

Resolved, That the Clerk communicate these resolutions to the Senate.

72

ADDRESS OF MR. MCMILLIN.

Mr. McMILLIN. Mr. Speaker, we assemble to-day to pay tribute to the memory of one of the most remarkable men ever produced by "the Volunteer State"—ISHAM GREEN HARRIS. Tennessee has been prolific of great men, and they have been prolific of great deeds. She, before admission to statehood, furnished John Sevier and his fellow-officers and their brave comrades to win the battle of Kings Mountain and the Revolution; furnished General Jackson to conquer England's trained army at New Orleans, and subsequently, as President, to stand as the great tribune of the people; furnished Polk to carry on the Mexican war; Houston to wrest Texas from Mexico; Crockett to immortalize "the Alamo" by his death, and Andrew Johnson to take the helm of state as President during the trying hours immediately succeeding our civil war. The State has furnished a long line of other noble and able statesmen, yet Mr. Speaker, ISHAM G. HARRIS stands out in history as a distinguished man, even when compared to these distinguished sons of our splendid State.

ISHAM G. HARRIS was born in Franklin County, Tenn., on the 10th of February, 1818. He died July 8, 1897. He therefore lacked but little of reaching fourscore years. He married Miss Martha Travis, of Paris, Tenn., whom he survived only a few months. They left four sons; and four of their children died before the parents.

That State—this country—has produced few men who achieved so many triumphs despite so many difficulties.

He was too poor when he began life to acquire a collegiate education. He was too poor even to start a business of his own and had to hire to another as clerk. But early in the action he showed those sterling qualities—intelligence, integrity, and industry—which caused him to win his first battle, enabled him to enter business on his own account about the time he attained his majority, and to triumph in so many of the battles of later life. But this is an experience so oft witnessed that it has come to be doubted whether poverty in youth has not made more great men than it ever marred. Poverty and misfortunes try the man. Trials and tribulations once passed are found to have chastened and strengthened the man instead of weakening him.

Mr. Speaker, a brief, plain narrative of the struggles of Senator HARRIS and his triumphs makes a very bright page in American history. He was born before Jefferson wrote his famous letter urging the promulgation of the " Monroe doctrine " or Monroe proclaimed it. He therefore saw the rise and triumph of that doctrine whereby our Government laid out the map of the world and forced the world to accept the map.

He was a young man when Jackson, who had been a soldier in the Revolution, still lived. He beheld his country when it numbered but a few millions; he lived to see it surpass in greatness and grandeur not only the nations now existing but any nation that ever rose in the world's history. He lived when there was not a railroad, a telegraph, or a telephone in the world. Yet when he died our country had enough railroad mileage to circle the globe six times. Before he died he could whisper across the State and talk almost across the continent. Before his death he could have recorded his voice in the graphophone so it could be taken off sigh for sigh and sound for sound by his grandchildren fifty years after his death.

As already stated, he moved from Franklin County, Tenn., to Henry County when only about 14 years old, to hire as a clerk in a store. I have narrated how he set up for himself at the age of 21 years.

But mercantile pursuits were not sufficiently exciting for him. While thus engaged, looking forward to a vocation more congenial with his fiery and eloquent nature, he had studied law at night, getting whatever private training he could obtain.

He moved back to Paris, Tenn., whence he had gone to Mississippi, and in the year 1841 began the practice of the law in conjunction with an older brother, who was both able and distinguished in the practice. From this time forward his life was one of strenuous exertion, constant battle, and great triumph.

He was elected a member of the State legislature from his senatorial district in 1847.

In 1848 he was a candidate for elector from his Congressional district on the Democratic ticket. He displayed tact and ability to such a degree as to arouse the enthusiasm of his friends and cause them to look to him for a standard bearer later on.

In 1849 he was nominated for Congress, again canvassing the district, and was elected.

He was reelected in 1851, and at the close of his term, declining further nomination, he removed to Memphis, which was his home until his death, and entered successfully into the practice of his profession.

In 1856 he again entered the political arena as candidate for elector for the State at large on the Democratic ticket. His opponent in this campaign was one of the most distinguished of Tennessee sons, ex-Governor Neil S. Brown, who was not only able as a lawyer but able in debate. He was one of two distinguished brothers, the other being Gen. John C. Brown, who were governors of Tennessee.

In 1857 he was elected governor of Tennessee.

In 1859 he was reelected.

Then came the stirring events of the civil war in which he was to play so distinguished a part. As "war governor" he was untiring in his exertions in organizing and equipping troops, sending them to the front, and in feeding and clothing them. So energetically and successfully did he carry on this work that when the war closed about 100,000 men had been furnished to the Confederate army, notwithstanding the thousands that had gone to the Union Army, the State being divided in sentiment on the question of secession.

When Tennessee was overrun by the Federal forces and the capitol had to be abandoned, Senator HARRIS took up his line of march with the Confederate troops and stayed with them to the close of the conflict. He was a portion of the time with that great cavalry commander, Gen. Bedford Forrest; but probably a greater portion of his time prior to the death of that distinguished general was spent with Gen. Albert Sidney Johnston, by whose side he was when that great commander of Confederate forces was killed as Shiloh. One of the most graphic descriptions I ever heard was by Senator HARRIS, only a few days before the beginning of his last illness, giving an account of the death of Gen. Albert Sidney Johnston and the great battle in which it occurred.

During this period he had in his custody the school fund of Tennessee. It was a coin fund, dedicated by the people of Tennessee to the cause of education alone, and amounted to many hundred thousand dollars. When compelled to leave the State he carried this treasure with him, and month after month and year after year, from city to city, as the army went, the fund was taken. Through all troubles it was preserved intact, and when the war closed, not being able to return to the State, he sent it back to be used as the law had dedicated it.

At the close of this fierce conflict, in which more than 2,000,000 soldiers had participated, sectional and war prejudices were at the highest pitch. The then ruling government of Tennessee, on the charge that he had been guilty of treason to the State, offered a reward for Senator HARRIS, by reason of which he left the United States and went to Mexico. After staying some time in Mexico he went to England, where he lived and engaged in business for one year. The prejudices of war subsiding, he returned to the State he had loved so well and resumed the practice of his profession.

He continued this, taking interest in the political affairs of his State, but seeking no office until 1876. In that year the Democratic party, in convention at Nashville, moved by a remarkably eloquent address delivered by him to the convention, nominated him over all opposition as candidate for elector on the Tilden-Hendricks ticket. It soon developed that there still existed in some portions of the State prejudice against him to such a degree that he came to believe that votes would be polled against his party on account of prejudices against him. With the same manliness and devotion that had characterized his whole life he came forward in a patriotic address to the people, declining to make the race for elector, in order that some man against whom there were no prejudices might be put forward by his party. At the same time he declared his purpose to be no laggard in the conflict, but to go forward, doing battle wherever his services were needed, which he did.

In 1877 he was elected by the Democratic legislature to the United States Senate, where the balance of his life was spent in faithful and efficient service to his country. Those who served with him in the Senate have already testified to his efficiency in every department of legislative life. It will, therefore, not be necessary for me to recount all of his characteristics in that body. Suffice it to say that as a debater he was courteous but bold, pointed, able, and eloquent. As a parliamentarian, he probably had no superior in the distinguished body of which he was a member. He adhered with unflinching devotion to the principles of the Democratic party. He believed in a strict construction of the Constitution, in economy in public expenses, and the exertion of the taxing power only for the purpose of obtaining revenue.

When the great conflict was on in 1894 for revising the tariff laws and reducing taxation to the requirements of economic government, he was made the manager in the Senate of that measure. He was also appointed one of the conferees on the part of the Senate when that bill was sent to conference. During the long and trying period that it was in conference he attended with the same punctuality and worked with the same assiduity that characterized him in all things. Though then very old, he was able to stand the long strain when others more youthful and apparently more robust gave way. He and the lamented and eloquent Voorhees were both on that conference, and have both gone hence, leaving behind a great name and record.

During a portion of the time that Senator HARRIS was a member of the Senate he was President pro tempore of that body, and no man was more frequently called to the chair, whether the administration of the Senate was of his political faith or not, than he.

Many regarded Senator HARRIS as impetuous. He was never so in coming to a conclusion. He was careful of his premises, deliberate in making up his mind; but when the conclusion was reached, his stand was so decided and his action so unrestrained that many, not knowing him well, would conclude that he was an impulsive and impetuous man, whereas nothing was further from him.

He was warm in his friendships, true to his friends, and truthful in all things. He never made a promise that he did not fulfill nor even give an intimation in a direction that he did not intend to go.

Blessed with a strong constitution that seemed to require no care, with a body that never tired, and a spirit that never flagged, this remarkable man moved on to a ripe old age with not a mental faculty dimmed and with none of his fiery spirit quenched. But the end came, as it must come to all. The time arrived when the spirit, though unimpaired, could not pull forward a weary, worn, and wasted body. Until a very recent period before his death he continued to wait upon the daily sessions of the Senate with his accustomed regularity. Finally, when the breakdown did come, he went to the seashore to gain strength and recuperation. And well might he, for during the period that they were contemporaries the waves had not been more ceaseless in their motion than his spirit ceaseless in its exertion. The recuperation obtained there was only temporary. He returned to the Capitol and to the Senate Chamber to again take up the struggle; but the effort was useless. The time had come when a long and eventful life must terminate—that earth was to reclaim its dust, and God the spirit He had lent it. I stood at his bedside and felt his last pulse beat. The end was as calm as the summer's eve on which it came. The man who had been so fiery in life was as a sleeping child in death.

With appropriate ceremonies his funeral occurred in the Senate Chamber. There is where it should have occurred. He had had every trial that could test youth, every struggle that could embarrass young manhood, and every difficulty that could hamper mature manhood and old age. Step by step he had gone forward and upward, till he had held almost every office in the gift of his State. And having been honored by it as few men are honored, he became an exile from it—a wanderer in foreign lands, where none but strange faces were to meet him and none but strange voices to greet him—a standing reward offered by his native State for his capture and return. But over all of these he triumphed, and returning to his loved Commonwealth, was again chosen as the leader of its thought and action, and for a fifth of a century occupied with distinguished ability a seat in that great Chamber. It was therefore fitting that the scene of his activities should be that of his funeral. The poverty under which he rested in his youth and the difficulties he encountered in after years neither retarded nor crushed him.

Mr. Speaker, it is said that the eagle builds its nest never near the ground, nor ever in the valley, but on loftiest and most inaccessible peaks. It is also said that when the parent bird concludes that the eaglets have lingered long enough around the nest she carries them, not down with tenderness and care to earth to try their wings, but bearing them aloft upon her back above the clouds she shakes them off in mid-air to defy the dangers and gain the glories of the skies. Like that young bird, our dead statesman was shaken off in tender years, but like the eagle, he soared above all difficulties.

Accompanied by a portion of his many faithful friends and associates, we took his remains to his native State. At the capitol the dead statesman, in the senate chamber where he had first had legislative experience, was visited by thousands. The men whom he had fought in past years and those with whom he had done battle alike came to pay the tribute of their respect to his memory. The old Confederate was there, the old Democrat, the aged Whig, the Republican—all were there, and there was no heart that was not sad. Thence his remains were taken to Memphis, and there thousands gathered to attend his funeral and to witness his burial. Near the great river, in the greatest of all the valleys of earth, in the beautiful cemetery of the splendid city of Memphis, we laid him to rest.

> Nor shall his glory be forgot
> While Fame her record keeps,
> Or memory points the hallowed spot
> Where valor proudly sleeps.

ADDRESS OF MR. BLAND.

Mr. BLAND. Mr. Speaker, the first acquaintance I had with the late Senator HARRIS was after he came to the Senate in 1877. Senator HARRIS was, I believe, for most of the time he was in the Senate, a member of the Finance Committee. During this time I was a member of the Committee on Coinage, Weights, and Measures in the House. The jurisdiction of these two committees often brought us in close relations personally and politically.

He became the leader of the Democratic party in the Senate in all the great battles for the free coinage of silver and in resisting the efforts of the opponents of bimetallism in further demonetizing it. During the great battle that is memorable in our history as probably one of the most notable in the annals of parliamentary debate that took place in the effort to repeal what is commonly known as the Sherman Act, the late Senator HARRIS took the leading part; in fact, he was, to all intents and purposes, the parliamentary counselor and leader in the Senate on the side of the bimetallists. I often saw him in the Senate when the questions of parliamentary law were raised during this contest take the leading part in maintaining the position of his side, and anyone who ever saw him in one of those contests, who had an opportunity to observe the great force with which he put his points and the clearness in which he stated his propositions and the strong and emphatic language in which he made his demonstrations, can never forget the power, both mental and physical, that was exhibited by the man. Every word came from him as a shot from a cannon, and it went to the mark as if aimed by an expert. There was no effort at ornate speech, but

S. Doc. 343——6

an immense cannonading of logic, power in statement, and conviction in argument.

I always regarded him as a firm and determined friend of the people as he understood their interests. He was a man who possessed great courage, and was not afraid to announce his views and opinions on any subject. He had that faith in the intelligence and fairness of the American people to believe that a man would be measured by them according to that degree of courage and fidelity with which he fought for the principles that he honestly maintained.

I shall not attempt to give a historical sketch of him, but shall leave that to those who knew him as a neighbor and friend from the State which he so long and ably represented not only in official positions at home but in the councils of the Federal Government. I shall not attempt to enter into a eulogy upon his high character. I could not pronounce a greater eulogy upon him than the simple truthful statement that from my knowledge of him, extending over a period of twenty years, he impressed me as a man of great ability and wide attainments; a man of undoubted courage and strong convictions, and was always ready to maintain them; that he was a true friend of constitutional liberty; that his heart went out to the great mass of American people, and it was their interest under the Constitution upon all economic questions that he brought all of his great ability to promote and subserve. His State has lost its greatest champion in the national councils; bimetallism has lost one of its most faithful advocates in the nation. His loss is felt not only in his State and throughout the nation as a great advocate of this cause, but is regretted by bimetallists throughout the world.

I speak especially on this question, because it was in the contests upon this subject that I became more intimately acquainted with him, and was enabled to form a just opinion of the man.

But his labors were confined to no particular subject. There was no great question of legislation affecting the interests of the people of his State and of the nation that he did not give to it his earnest attention, and upon all the subjects of the currency, tariff, of Federal and State control, of the rights and powers of the States as contradistinguished from the powers of the Federal Government; in other words, the great dividing line between these jurisdictions received his earnest investigation. He was sincerely a strict constructionist as it is understood and taught by such leaders as Jefferson and Calhoun and others of the party to which Senator Harris belonged. His discussions of these subjects were marked by great ability and zeal. He was a leader naturally. He towered above the average man, and by his will power and ability inspired confidence in those around him as a leader; hence he was a leader in the Senate, and to say that he took a leading part in that body is to pay a high tribute to his qualities as a great man.

Peace to his ashes; honor to his memory.

ADDRESS OF MR. RICHARDSON.

Mr. RICHARDSON. Mr. Speaker, when Senator ISHAM G. HARRIS died I felt a sense of personal loss such as I never realized before in the death of a public man. He was not only my political friend, but my intimate personal friend. In his death, therefore, I was conscious of the fact that while the country had suffered the loss of a valued public servant whose place could not well be filled, that personally I had lost one to whom I had been accustomed to look for that counsel and advice which only a true friend can give. I had known him from my boyhood. The first time I ever saw him I remember well. It was in 1856, when I, a mere youth, went to my county town to listen to a joint debate between himself and ex-Governor Neil S. Brown, of our State. They were the electors for the State at large that year, he representing Mr. Buchanan while Governor Brown represented Mr. Fillmore.

I next saw him the following year, when he was a candidate for governor of Tennessee, and had for his opponent Robert Hatton. Two years later, as a candidate for reelection to the office of governor, I witnessed the joint debate between himself and his Whig opponent, John Netherland. He was successful in both these campaigns for governor, and was renominated by his party for that office in 1861. During that year as a candidate I heard him in joint debate with his opponent, William H. Polk, a younger brother of President Polk. Inheriting as I did the political sentiments and theories of my father, who belonged to the old Whig party, I of course did not agree with Governor HARRIS in the opinions he gave expression to and in the arguments he made in those several joint debates which I have mentioned.

While I did not agree with him, I was greatly impressed by him as I observed his intense zeal, his fiery eloquence, his earnest gesture, and at times impassioned flights of oratory. The impressions I derived from his speeches, boy as I was, and fighting against them as I did by reason of the inherited opposition thereto, to which I have referred, made lodgment in my mind which was never eradicated. I shall not undertake to follow the career of this great man through all his public life in our State. Others have done this in their eulogies of him, which will appear along with my own.

He was born in Franklin County, Tenn., February 10, 1818. This county I had the honor to represent upon this floor for eight years, though it is not now within my district. At an early age he removed to Henry County, Tenn., where his parents died and are buried. Soon after his death many of the people of that county met in Paris, the county seat, where he had grown to manhood and practiced law, to pay tribute to his memory. A graceful and loving tribute was then and there paid to him by his former neighbors and friends. I take the liberty of using the resolutions they adopted for certain facts in his life and that of his family, which I set forth below. He was the son of Isham G. Harris and wife, Lucy Davidson Harris, and was the youngest son of a family of nine children. His oldest brother, George W. D. Harris, was an able and eloquent minister of the Methodist Episcopal Church. His brother William R. Harris was on the supreme bench of Tennessee at the time of his death, which occurred on the 19th of June, 1858, from the explosion of a steamboat boiler on the Mississippi River. Another brother, James Harris, a gallant Confederate soldier, fell at the battle of Shiloh in April, 1862.

Senator HARRIS went to Paris, Tenn., at the age of about 14 years, and began to work as a salesman in a dry goods store.

Three years later he went to Mississippi and engaged in merchandising in partnership with his brother. After about three years he sold out his interest in the store and was paid in the notes of a Mississippi bank and returned to Paris with the intention of studying law. The Mississippi bank failed, leaving him penniless, and he again engaged in merchandising, studying law at night until the year 1841, when he sold his interest in the business and entered upon the study of the law. Having applied himself closely to his studies while in business, he very early secured license and entered upon the practice. He was admitted to the bar at the May term of the court in 1841. He became at once a successful practitioner, taking rank as one of the best lawyers of the State.

He was married in 1843 to Miss Martha Travis, of which marriage there were born a family of eight children, four of whom survive. In 1847 he was elected to the State senate of Tennessee and in 1849 to a seat on this floor. He was reelected in 1851, and was again nominated in 1853, but declined the nomination and removed to Memphis that he might find a larger field in which to practice his profession. He continued in active practice until 1857, when, as I have stated he was chosen governor of Tennessee. He was the governor of our State from 1857 until the war between the States closed. He took a very active part in behalf of the Southern States during that war, participating in many battles.

After the establishment of peace he went to Mexico, where he remained about two years, going from there to London, where he remained until November, 1867. He then returned to Memphis and again entered upon the practice of law with great success. In 1876 the State convention placed him at the head of the electoral ticket of his party in Tennessee. His selection to this position did not meet with universal favor in one section of the State. He thereupon resigned as elector, but proceeded to make a thorough and extensive canvass of the whole State for his party. By this course and conduct he added great popularity to himself, and at the close of the canvass announced his candidacy for the United States Senate. When the legislature assembled the following January he was chosen Senator almost unanimously. He was reelected a Senator in 1883, in 1889, and in 1895.

I shall not attempt to discuss his long career in the Senate of the United States, but it is well known of all men that he adorned the position and met every requirement of the high trust with which he was clothed with earnestness, fidelity, and signal ability. He was a great debater, a faithful public servant, and a courageous soldier. He was the foremost man in Tennessee politics during his generation. He possessed fine conversational powers, and was a most entertaining companion. His manner was sometimes severe and apparently cross, but within him there was always sympathy and love for humanity. It has been truly said of him that more people are indebted to him for favors extended than to any other man who ever occupied a public office.

Mr. Speaker, his death was a great national calamity. For more than fifty years he served his country in the State and national councils. He held the highest stations the people of his State could give him. He had opportunities to accumulate wealth, but died poor. He was scrupulously honest in private life and incorruptible in the public service. He had all the courage of the most courageous, and would have gone to the stake rather than yield his convictions of right or duty. He was never of those who would follow a multitude to do evil. He was ambitious, but was not sordid or venal. He loved the people, but was in no sense a demagogue.

His character was positive and admitted of no compromise. He was always frank and sincere. He was either for you or against you. He either favored your measure or opposed it. You were never in doubt as to whether he favored you and your measure, for guile and deceit were strangers to him. He was the chief architect and builder of Tennessee's Democracy and the place he occupied in their hearts can not be filled. His integrity was never assailed nor questioned, and no man ever accused him of breaking a pledge or violating a promise. From early manhood through a long life and an honorable career, clothed oftentimes with trusts of the highest character, frequently taxed to the utmost of his physical endurance, his course had been steadily and unfalteringly upward. His candor, his faithfulness, his sagacity, his probity, with his integrity, honesty, courage, devotion to duty, and his successful career entitle his fame to endure and give conspicuous luster to Tennessee.

ADDRESS OF MR. MEYER OF LOUISIANA.

Mr. MEYER of Louisiana. Mr. Speaker, Senator ISHAM G. HARRIS, of Tennessee, whose memory we now meet to commemorate, was in every way a remarkable man.

He was born in Franklin County, Tenn., in 1818.

Sprung from Revolutionary stock, a country-bred boy, he had no special advantages of wealth, education, or family influence. He was the architect of his own fortune.

At the early age of 14 years, with only a country-school education, he began the battle of life.

Leaving his home, he settled at Paris, Tenn., hired himself as a merchant's clerk; next entered on business for his own account, and meantime studied law at night; then finally graduated, went to the bar, and began the practice of law at Paris. His great industry and energy, which as a business man made him successful, soon made him preeminent in his chosen profession.

The attractions of the political field in a country where the people actively control prevailed over the habits and inducements of legal pursuits. His advancement here was rapid. In 1846 he was elected to the State legislature; next behold him the candidate for Presidential elector in his Congressional district; then elected and reelected to the House; then in 1853 declining reelection; next, Presidential elector; then in 1857 elected governor of the State of Tennessee, reelected in 1859, and again in 1861.

Honors such as these, worthily won, might well fill the measure of any man's ambition, but these honors were only the prelude to a career which for nearly forty years since has made him conspicuous.

He was the great war governor of the State of Tennessee;

organized two thousand volunteers for the Confederate service; took his own full share of the perils of battle, led a regiment into the bloody field of Shiloh; stood by Gen. Albert Sidney Johnston, the great Confederate commander, when he received his mortal wound; carried him from the field; and served for three years more as aid on the staffs of the generals who successively commanded the Confederate army of Tennessee.

At the close of the war he was for years an exile by reason of his distinction and services to his State, which made him a special mark for slander and malignity. But when, in 1867 the abatement of passion finally permitted the step, he returned to Memphis, where he again practiced law for ten years.

In 1877 he was elected a Senator of the United States from the State of Tennessee, taking his seat March 5, 1877. He was reelected in 1883; again in 1889, and finally in 1895, for the term of six years. On the 8th of July last he passed away, full of years and full of honors.

Such a succession of public honors was not the result of accident, nor of pertinacity in seeking public trusts. More than once he declined public station for private pursuits. He was a man of convictions, fearless, bold, uncompromising, and took all risks in times of conflict, strife, disorder, violent prejudice, and strong excitement. If, therefore, we find such a constant and unvaried tide of success, we must study the causes in the intellectual and moral force of the man.

Pursuing this pathway, I find no difficulty in locating the cause of his success and popularity. He did not inherit fortune, nor did he ever acquire any large means. He showed grit and determination at the very beginning. He had excellent business habits; he had the qualities of action—the executive faculty.

He had quickness of perception, and, what is far more quickness of decision. He had energy, industry, close application, persistence, and the ambition to succeed in everything he undertook.

These qualities told on everything he did. They are largely the secret of his success as merchant, lawyer, governor, politician, and Congressman. Perhaps the most trying time of his life was as governor of Tennessee from 1861 to 1865, and the two or three years of exile and straitened means that followed the war. But while adversity might come, he was not the man to lie down and surrender. His nature was heroic. He triumphed over adverse fate. The personal and moral heroism that bore him to the field of Shiloh and through the perils of the war marked his entire career. In peace and in war he was a born fighter and a leader of men.

He exercised marked influence upon his associates and contemporaries. He did not carry Tennessee out of the Union, as some would say, but he led in the movement, and gave it much of its strength.

The same influence was witnessed in his career in Congress.

He was not a great or a learned lawyer. He had given too much time to other things to fill a rôle that is only filled by those who give their whole lives to that arduous, zealous profession of the law: but he was a good business lawyer. His success at the bar can not be otherwise explained.

He was a clear-headed, logical man, and never neglected what he had on hand. As a speaker in the Senate he might not, indeed, be eloquent. His style did not smell of the lamp. He did not often speak at length. He did not speak for the sake of display or merely to make a speech: but when he did speak he was forcible, clear, strong, and convincing. He went at once to the turning point of the case. He wasted no words. He struck fairly at the shield of his antagonist. He had the ability, it he pleased, to discuss profound and difficult economic questions. His speech some years ago upon the silver question was regarded as one of the best of that long and able debate in the Senate.

Very soon after he came to the Senate Senator HARRIS was placed on very important committees, which he filled up to the time of his death. But while a hard working, business Senator, he gave special attention to parliamentary law. He was made President pro tempore of the body, and very often occupied the chair. He enjoyed it, and the Senators of both parties were glad to have him sit there. They all knew that he was absolutely fair, impartial, and always courteous and conservative.

The knowledge of parliamentary law, and, above all, the ability to preside, is a rare gift. It is a great, a responsible trust to be the presiding officer of the Senate or the House of Representatives; and one who worthily, ably, and conscientiously fills such a trust has rendered a most important service to the body over which he presides and to the cause of representative government, upon which our public liberties depend.

In private life Senator HARRIS was a simple, natural man. His sincerity and frankness were his most striking qualities, but he was also kindly and genial. He did not go out of his way to conciliate foes, but he was rarely aggressive, almost always conciliatory, and to his friends was true as steel.

I have said he was a man of convictions. He was always a Democrat. He was true to his party, and never went back on his flag. He abhorred treachery or duplicity in politics. But while a strong party man, his political foes felt that he would never strike them unfairly. They respected and honored him. They never doubted his word or questioned his integrity.

After a long life, in peace and in war, filling many trying positions, this plain man of the people, simple, natural, strong, heroic, has passed from our midst, with no stain on his record, no page of his life that his friends would wish to blot; honored and mourned by his State, and by all who had the good fortune to know him. I count it a high privilege to pay this last tribute of my respect to one on whose career I would willingly dwell longer if the work had not been so well performed by others.

ADDRESS OF MR. McRAE.

Mr. McRAE. Mr. Speaker, the eloquent, affectionate, and interesting eulogies to which we have listened make it unnecessary for me to say more than to testify my personal regard and reverence for the great statesman and Democratic leader whose memory we commemorate to-day. He deserves all of the encomiums bestowed upon him here or elsewhere.

In many respects he was one of the most remarkable men that this country has ever produced. His life was a success, and yet full of struggle and adventure. We first hear of him as an ambitious, penniless youth of 14 years, struggling against those dread jailers of the human heart, humble birth and poverty. At 21 a successful country merchant; at 25 a good lawyer; at 30 a leader of his party in the State legislature; at 32 a Representative in Congress, and at 40 governor of his State. He served through the late war as governor of Tennessee, and at the same time on the staff of Gen. Albert Sidney Johnston until the death of the general at Shiloh.

The success of the Union Army made him an exile from the home of his birth and the people he loved. After more than two years in Mexico and England, he returned to Memphis broken in fortune and began again the practice of his profession. As soon as the people of his native State were allowed to control their elections and vote, the Democrats of that State turned to him as their leader. In 1877 he was elected to the United States Senate, where he served the State until his death. He lived almost fourscore years, and held office for nearly fifty years.

At the end of a career so remarkable and eventful it is proper that the Congress of which he was a member should temporarily suspend its ordinary labors to pay tribute to his character and find, if possible, the great secret of his wonderful success. He was without college education and was an entire stranger to the artful practices of the politician, but he possessed a strong, well-balanced mind and from childhood was not ashamed to work, not afraid to tell the truth, and in everything was direct and honest.

In boyhood, in manhood, in private transactions, in public life, in military life, in adversity, in prosperity, in his own country, or in exile, his personal integrity and superb courage never failed him. He was true to himself. He was true to every trust reposed in him—to his State, his constituents, and to his friends. He was courteous and candid to his foes. He trusted the people; they had faith in him. He never betrayed them; they never deserted him. He died comparatively poor in purse, but rich in that which above everything else he desired, the love and confidence of the people of this Republic and particularly those of Tennessee.

ADDRESS OF MR. BENTON.

Mr. BENTON. Mr. Speaker, the first name of a public man that I ever learned to utter was that of ISHAM G. HARRIS, or as he was familiarly known in our section of Tennessee, GREEN HARRIS. I was born a constituent of his. He was the first public man I ever heard on the hustings. I come of a family that did not originally lean to Mr. HARRIS'S views. It was after the decay of the Whig party began, in 1854, that my father and uncles (declining to become members of the Know-Nothing party) joined fortunes with HARRIS. So that my memories of him began as a political opponent, but early ripened into those of a political friend and leader.

The most remarkable thing to my mind as a child was the fascination the man had for me. I always attended, when I had permission, the public speakings in my own county, and especially asked the privilege of hearing Governor HARRIS. His head looked to me in those days exceedingly large. He was bald when yet a very young man. His eyes set deep back in his head and, when animated in debate, were searching and commanding. He was not what we call an eloquent man after the manner of Haskell and Haynes and Henry, yet there was a peculiarity about his expressions, a directness, as if in a steady charge, that absolutely fascinated me as a child, and I can remember well, when I would go home from a meeting, that I insisted upon explanations being made to me of what was meant by certain of his arguments.

I remember, as well as if they were yesterday, his great debates in the fifties, with Governor Brown, General Hatton, and Colonel Netherland, his discussions of "squatter sovereignty" and the " Kansas and Nebraska bills," and the attitude which he demanded Tennessee should maintain (questions of which I as a child could have no understanding), but I was so interested by the manner and force of the man that I was compelled to inquire the subject of his talk.

I can remember well when he first became a candidate for governor and came into our section of the State. It was a remarkable campaign; perhaps not so remarkable as the campaign just before it, in 1856, when he defeated Governor Brown for elector at large, but from the standpoint of national politics more important and far-reaching than the great debates between Johnson and Henry and Johnson and Gentry. But in our section of the State it was more important than either of those campaigns I have mentioned. HARRIS was our idol, our political leader. To our section of the State he was neighbor and friend, and we were greatly interested in the outcome of the campaign. The men with whom he debated these questions in 1856 and 1857 and 1859 were men of the finest character and the highest ability and education, and it was a subject of conversation and comment among the educated and accomplished Tennesseans that HARRIS always held his own with the most accomplished and best learned of the public men of his day.

As has been before stated, he was what, for the lack of a better definition, we call a "self-made" man. That is to say, he was without a college education. He had not been trained by any literary master. He had a little of what we call academy education. He commenced life without means and without being well equipped in college; but I am told by his confrères that he was a student of men and events rather than of books, though as a youth he read books. I well recollect hearing a conversation in the cloakroom here last winter, by the only man who ever held a successful tilt with him in politics, Emerson Etheridge, that it was commonly known in Henry County in his boyhood days that every book bearing upon public questions which could possibly be borrowed or bought HARRIS read; and while he lacked college training, he gave all of his spare time to informing himself on the great questions of the day. And when he came out into public life, it was a cause of marvel among the prominent men of the State that on all the questions of interest of that day he stood in the forefront.

I believe, Mr. Speaker, that I do no violence to the glory roll of Tennessee when I say that next to General Jackson ISHAM G. HARRIS was the most potential figure that has ever lived in that State. He had at one period of his life bitter and resentful enemies. A man of his positive character always has; but up against them he had the most powerful, positive, and affectionate friends of any man who has lived in the State of Tennessee since I can remember. To him, to his force of character, to his indomitable energy, to his tremendous courage, to his incisive arguments, more than to any other man, and I may say than to all other men of the State, is due the position which Tennessee assumed in 1861.

In 1860 the Democratic party of the State was divided. He and Senator Johnson at that time both supported Mr. Breckinridge. Early in the year 1861 they separated. Governor HARRIS insisted that the election of Mr. Lincoln would lead to the destruction of State sovereignty and centralization of government. Taking the resolutions of 1798 as his text and Mr. Calhoun as his political guide, he demanded that the State of Tennessee should follow her sister States of the South. In this contention he was met and resisted by the most powerful Democrat then living in the State, Senator Johnson, afterwards President, who led the Union element in the Democratic party. He was met by that other powerful element, the remnants of the old Whig party, led by Brownlow, of East Tennessee, and M. R. Hill and Emerson Etheridge, of West Tennessee, all of them the brainiest and bravest of men.

In the first contest, in February, 1861, an election was held for delegates to a constitutional convention, as well as to test the sense of the people on the question of secession. The advocates of secession were defeated by more than 60,000 majority. But Governor HARRIS was not dismayed. Under his undaunted leadership those who believed that Tennessee should join the South kept up the fight. He called the legislature to meet in special session. In this connection I desire to call attention to his justly celebrated message to the general assembly of Tennessee.

At this period, Mr. Speaker, far removed as we are from those troublous times of civil war, when we can speak of the public questions of that period with calmness and without being offensive, I may be permitted to call attention to his message to the general assembly of Tennessee in the spring of 1861. I do not believe I ever read a state paper on the sovereignty of the States, or the original doctrine of "State rights," as it was understood by our school of politics, that was in all of its elements so strong, convincing, and conclusive as that message.

In aid of his irresistible arguments, his energy and his courage were so intense that in spite of the fact that Tennessee had voted in February, 1861, by a majority of 60,000 to remain in the Union, in less than six months the State of Tennessee joined her fortunes with the South and became a member of the Confederacy. My attention was not called to Governor HARRIS's message in a serious way until after the war. I procured a copy of the acts of the general assembly and have it in my library, and once in a while I read it, more because of the strength of the paper than in memory of its subject. And I say to-day that in my opinion it is the most powerful argument ever made from that standpoint.

Governor HARRIS's distinctive characteristics were "honesty of purpose" and "directness of speech." He was a positive and affirmative man. He was quick to decide, and forceful and lucid in explaining his position. His worst enemy never declared of him that there was any doubt about where he stood upon any public question. Public men, as we know, nearly all at some time bend to public opinion and give up cherished views, but Governor HARRIS fought with the same degree of courage public opinion, when he thought it was wrong, as when he was leading in the current running his way. He fought and won with public opinion against him in 1849, 1856, and 1861. And his last great battle was for bimetallism against a strong current.

He did not study to ascertain the popular side. He only waited to convince himself of what was right for the people and constitutional. Then he spoke and acted. Secession was as unpopular in 1860 and early in 1861 in Tennessee as it was in Illinois. But it did not deter him. He believed that the reserved rights of the States were to be invaded and the Constitution violated, and he acted accordingly. The general belief in his honesty of purpose and his force of character, together with his powerful arguments, made Tennessee a part of the Confederacy.

There is a potent lesson to young ambition in the life of Senator HARRIS. He was honest—honest in thought, honest in speech, honest in private life. His word to his neighbor was sufficient. This made him strong with the people. And he believed in the people. Like his great political master, Jefferson, he trusted the people, and they in turn trusted him. I knew Governor HARRIS well in my boyhood days. He was

often in my town. I lived within a stone's throw of his illustrious brother, Rev. George W. D. Harris, one of the strongest
and most distinguished men in the Southern Methodist Church.

Force of character and integrity of purpose is and was in the
name. It has been said of the HARRIS name that there was no
compromise in them. It has been stated often that the dead
Senator was dogmatic. Mr. Speaker, what man of strong mind,
great force of character, information, and positive convictions
but what is more or less dogmatic? And yet with all, this great
forceful, driving man, when properly approached, was as gentle
as a woman. I was not taught to regard Governor HARRIS as
a jurist of equal merit with his brother, Judge William Harris,
or Judge William B. Turley. But he was a very successful
practitioner of the law. His character for honesty, his forceful
and positive way of approaching everything made him a success
at the bar. He did not study rhetorical art, hence did not rank
with the orators of Tennessee. He did not delve deeply into
the philosophy of the law, so as to become a great judge, for,
as has been well said by the gentleman from Louisiana [Mr.
Meyer], "the law is an exceedingly jealous mistress, and will
not permit her votaries to become great who worship at any
other shrine." Yet, Mr. Speaker, Governor HARRIS was one
of the best lawyers I have ever known who was also a successful politician.

While he was not a great orator, he had that character of
speech which is the best eloquence. He persuaded men to his
way of thinking by his integrity of intention and his simple but
forceful expression. He was a successful politician without
veiling any of his opinions. ISHAM G. HARRIS was more than
a politician. He was a statesman. That splendid term as
applied to him is deserved. He believed that the fathers of the
Republic builded the Constitution to guard the rights and

contribute to the happiness of the people, and so believing he was a "strict constructionist." His last struggle was to restore to the people "bimetallism," their constitutional right. He spoke that which he thought; he acted his convictions; he thought not for himself but for his people. Of such are statesmen. History will say that all in all ISHAM GREEN HARRIS was one of the very strongest men that have ever lived in the State of my nativity.

ADDRESS OF MR. RHEA OF KENTUCKY.

Mr. RHEA of Kentucky. Mr. Speaker, in the public life of this country, no man has more fully and honorably left the imprint of his character and great ability than ISHAM G. HARRIS. For half a century and more he stood in the fierce light of the public gaze, and the universal judgment of his fellow-citizens vindicates the integrity of his actions and bears testimony to his honesty and manhood. In all the affairs of life, in all its walks, as the private citizen, as the public servant, his qualities of heart and mind have vindicated the purity of his motives and the high purposes that ever impelled his intercourse with his fellowmen.

With that great State, Tennessee, that so long recognized and valued his worth, and which he so long honored as State official and in the larger sphere of Federal public service, his name is inseparably linked. And whether in the discharge of his duties as a State official or the broader arena of Federal legislation, a wisdom and fidelity not surpassed and rarely equaled have marked his public career. A singleness of purpose, guided by the best interests of all the people, as he could understand and know them, was the rule of his life.

For a brief time, laying aside the duties of civil station to enter into the more stirring scenes and activities of warfare, the same high resolves and purposes, the same fidelity to duty as he saw it, guided his feet. He saw his people divided—the North against the South. He cast his fortunes with the people of that sun-kissed land that gave him birth and whose rights, as he believed, were assailed. When this darkest page in our country's history was closed, when the cause for which he fought was lost, when the starry banner of the Union floated once more over a reunited country, the roar of cannon, the rattle of musketry, the gleam of sabers had ceased, this man, accepting the issues as settled, in good faith did what he could to heal the breaches made by war and to set in motion again the forces of civil government for the upbuilding of our common country. Broad gauged, liberal minded, he still admired the beauty of the Southern Cross, but its effulgence did not in his eyes dim the brilliancy of the Northern Star. Reaching a ripe old age, the sands of life run out. He slept. How well he met the obligations of life, with what fidelity and integrity he discharged them, the judgment of the present is known, the history of the future will record—

In his honor impregnable,
In his simplicity sublime;
No cause ever had a nobler defender,
No principle a purer victim.

ADDRESS OF MR. BROWNLOW.

Mr. BROWNLOW. Mr. Speaker, one who, at the assembling of this Congress in extra session, had, in the coordinate House of Congress, by more than twenty years' service become a familiar presence, a potent influence, came not again on our reassembling. We are paying the last tribute of respect to one who served longer in the Senate of the United States than has any citizen of my State, and whose name will be forever prominently associated with her history.

ISHAM GREEN HARRIS played a leading and bold part in every prominent national measure for the past forty-seven years. He was a very remarkable man and of a family remarkable for intellect, one of his brothers having been distinguished as a judge of Tennessee's highest court and another as a strong, forceful clergyman of the Methodist Church. With educational advantages scarcely worthy of the name, he possessed a felicity, fluency, and vigor of speech possessed by few collegians. His will power was phenomenal.

Whether as an advocate before a jury, as a representative in this body during the stormy period of 1850, as governor of Tennessee organizing and planning for the secession of that old Whig, antisecession State from our Federal Union, organizing and equipping an army, conducting a political campaign in his own State, or organizing for the free-silver campaign of 1896, he threw himself into all his undertakings with that determination and utter disregard of obstacles which are usually guaranties of success.

From his entrance into public life when a very young man he was the acknowledged leader of his party in western Tennessee.

When Andrew Johnson had nearly completed a second term as governor of Tennessee in 1857, the Democratic party with one voice turned to HARRIS as their most capable leader, and nominated him for governor; and on the threshold of the successful canvass he then made an incident occurred illustrative of his character.

Mr. Johnson had prepared a speech which he intended delivering and circulating in pamphlet form. HARRIS was asked by him to hear this speech read, with the remark that " he intended it as the keynote to the approaching campaign." After Johnson had read his speech to HARRIS, the latter said: " I should regret to have you deliver that speech as a 'keynote to this campaign.'" "Why?" asked Johnson. "Because," said HARRIS, "my competitor will be sure to read from it in our joint discussions." "What if he does?" asked Johnson. "Then," replied HARRIS, " I would denounce it, and, from your and my position in our party, it would be very embarrassing to not only ourselves but to our party. In that speech, Johnson, you advocate a new basis of representation in Congress and the Electoral College, eliminating the three-fifths of the slave population now represented, and you advocate changes in the Federal Constitution by which the President, Vice-President, United States Senators, and the entire Federal judiciary shall be elected by a direct vote of the people, and the judiciary for a limited period. Not one of your propositions can be found in any platform of the Democratic party, State or national. I am opposed to all of them. They are not Democracy; they are only Andy Johnsonisms, and you can not force them on me as a keynote for my campaign."

For the first time Mr. Johnson encountered within his party a will as imperious as his own. He was ardently desirous of the election of a legislature which would make him Senator, and as the Whigs had elected the three previous legislatures he felt compelled to yield to the younger leader to prevent division in his party, and he failed to deliver the speech he had prepared. But there was never any cordial feeling after this between the two leaders. Had not Johnson been accustomed to the unquestioning obedience of the politicians of his party he would not have made the mistake of trying to put his collar over the neck of his younger confrère. He would have remembered that HARRIS was almost the only Democrat of influence in Tennessee who had dared oppose Mr. Clay's compromise measures of 1850 in the face of the overwhelming sentiment of the people of that State in favor of their adoption.

In 1859 and 1861 he was reelected governor of his State, which office he held till the close of the late war, and from the inauguration of the rebellion of 1861 until his death his supremacy was as absolute in his party in Tennessee as was ever that of Andrew Jackson and Andrew Johnson, and lasted longer than that of either. Johnson's began with his election as governor in 1853 and terminated in 1861, when he patriotically refused to follow his party and State into rebellion. True, he was elected to the Senate in 1875 by a majority of only 1 vote, but a majority of his party voted against him because he had opposed it on the war question, and because of this ground of opposition the Republicans in the legislature voted for and elected him. The supremacy of Andrew Jackson in Tennessee politics began in 1815, with his superb victory at New Orleans, and terminated in 1836, when the people of the State became weary of worthless "wild-cat" local bank money and free trade. Johnson's domination in his party was for a period of eight, Jackson's twenty-one, and HARRIS's thirty-six years and until his death.

Of the large number of able men in the executive chairs of

the States, North and South, with the inauguration of war in 1861, no one of them was possessed of more determination than the governor of Tennessee, or of as much executive ability, except the great and lamented war governor of Indiana, Oliver P Morton. It was the expression of the London Times that the most plausible justification of the reasons for the action of the seceding States was made by Governor HARRIS in his messages to the legislature of Tennessee in 1861. Unsound and sophistical as I regard his reasoning to have been, it is a fact that in the labor demanded of him as the governor of a State reluctant to secede, and divided in sentiment as Tennessee was, he showed such herculean energy as to entitle him to a position among the first of the forceful men of that era of forceful men. What Governor Morton was to his State and the Federal Government, that was Governor HARRIS to Tennessee and the ill-fated Confederacy.

At no time did he shrink from any responsibility, however perilous; any labor, however arduous. Although prior to the election of Mr. Lincoln he was recognized in Tennessee as the ablest man of his party except Andrew Johnson, yet it was as governor of that State he became a national figure. The rapidity with which he organized 120,000 men for the Confederate army, despite the fact that 40,000 Tennesseeans enlisted in the Union Army, stamps him as a man of extraordinary executive ability. In an account of the battle of Shiloh, by Col. William Preston Johnston, son of Albert Sidney, in the Century Magazine for February, 1885, the writer says his father's army "was weakened by the necessity of keeping thousands of troops in East Tennessee to overawe the Union population of that section, so as to guard the only line of railroad communication between Virginia and Tennessee."

He says further, "This hostile section penetrated the heart of the Confederacy like a wedge and flanked and weakened General Johnston's line of defense, requiring as it did constant vigilance and repression.'' And he adds that, of all the executives in the vast territory, ''an empire in extent,'' constituting the department of Albert Sidney Johnston, ''the only governor who furnished his State's quota of troops was Governor HARRIS, of Tennessee.'' These words are in reply to the criticisms of General Johnston by Southern newspapers for the loss of Forts Henry and Donaldson and the retreat of the Confederate army from Bowling Green and Nashville, and were intended as a vindication of that distinguished officer, but it will be seen that they are at the same time a high tribute to the executive ability of Governor HARRIS and to the unflinching loyalty and heroism of the Union patriots of East Tennessee, with whom the Governor had to contend.

Nor were Senator HARRIS's activities confined to recruiting a large army. During nearly the entire war he served as an aid on the staffs of the various commanders of the leading Confederate army of the Southwest, periling his life for a cause he deemed just—a feature of his character wherein he differed from nearly all the political leaders who aided in precipitating the civil war, for history records that these gentlemen almost invariably preferred bombproof positions to the perils of the battlefield. Had he chosen arms for his profession he might have made a great general, and rivaled the fame of that distinguished soldier, Gen. Joseph E. Johnston, on whose staff he served. Whatever Generals N. B. Forrest, William B. Bate, B. F. Cheatham, John C. Brown, and others did for the military fame of Tennessee and for their mistaken cause is largely to be shared by their coadjutor, the chief magistrate of Tennessee. And to the arbitrary and herculean labors of Governor HARRIS to force the highlanders of East Tennessee into a service abhorrent to their consciences is largely to be attributed the most heroic and sublime manifestation of physical and moral courage and patriotism recorded in the annals of American history.

But when this "man of blood and iron" attempted the coercion of the descendants of the heroes of Kings Mountain and New Orleans he encountered a people whose courage and determination were equal to his own, and who so far from yielding to his imperious will, backed up as it was with regiments and brigades, furnished to the Union Army a larger number of soldiers, in proportion to population, than any section of the United States; and I take pride in stating that I represent a district whose quota to the Federal Army of white soldiers exceeded that of any district in the Union. And these loyal heroes and their leaders, Generals Samuel P. Carter, Joseph A. Cooper, Alvan C. Gillem, James P. Brownlow, and others did as much for the military fame of Tennessee as did the heroes and their leaders of the opposing side; and after Tennessee's vast mineral and other resources shall have been developed under free labor, the verdict of impartial history will be that they loved their State as well and served it better. Thus from the crosses of war came the heroes who have shed imperishable fame on Tennessee. "Wine issues from the trodden grape; iron is blistered into steel."

With the downfall of the ill-fated Confederacy, for whose success he had performed such herculean labors, Governor HARRIS retired from participation in public life until in October, 1869, when he came to Nashville to aid in the defeat for the United States Senate of his old rival and enemy, Andrew Johnson. With the termination of the war an incident occurred illustrative of Senator HARRIS's personal integrity in connection with the public funds of the State, and I give the facts somewhat in detail because they have been distorted and misrepresented by certain of his political and personal opponents and in turn by those who would do injustice to Republicans.

The school fund of Tennessee in 1862 amounted to $2,679,-018.33, all deposited in and constituting a part of the assets of the Bank of Tennessee. In 1862 the Confederate legislature of the State directed that this fund should be invested in Confederate bonds, and it was so invested. That was an end of the Tennessee antebellum school fund, as at the close of the war the Confederate bonds were without value. In these assets, before they were removed south on the approach of Buell's army to Nashville, was $720,380.94 in coin. The fact that the reports of the bank on January 1, 1862, showed this sum in coin among the assets is probably the basis of the unintentionally untruthful statement that has been often published that $700,000 of the assets were turned over to the State authorities in 1865 and wasted. But the truth is the coin so turned over amounted to only $446,719.70. Part of the original sum was paid in salaries of State officers, part of it loaned before its return to Nashville, as the receipts in the boxes showed. These receipts and memoranda accounted for the difference between the $720,380.94 in coin, as shown by the report of January 1, 1862, and $446,719.70, the amount returned to Nashville and turned over to the State authorities in 1865, less the necessary expenses incident to their return to Nashville.

By act of the legislature of January 9, 1865, the governor, secretary of state, and comptroller were directed to invest the coin so returned, the $446,719.70, for the benefit of the school fund. In obedience to that act 7-30 United States bonds were bought, and the premium on gold being large at that time, the bonds purchased amounted to $618,250. These bonds were in the custody of the State treasurer, R. L. Stanford. In violation of the law, which required that they be kept at Nashville, he deposited them in a Memphis national bank which subsequently failed. When the action of the treasurer became known, the governor, by authority of the legislature, sent a committee to Memphis which recovered for the State $368,433.85. How much of the remainder, $249,816.15, has been recovered, I can not say, as there has not been a final termination of some litigation growing out of the matter. The treasurer, when detected in his violation of law in sending these bonds away from the capital, was the president of a Johnson political club in opposition to the reconstruction policy of Congress. He was not a Republican or ex-Confederate. He had been an officer in the Federal Army, and owed his election as treasurer to the influence of his personal and political friend, President Andrew Johnson. When his offense was made public the treasurer committed suicide. The probabilities are he had not intended to become a defaulter. He thought to speculate on State funds without the State losing by it.

When the war ended, Senator HARRIS left the United States, going first to Mexico and then to England. In 1866 he returned to Tennessee. Had he not been an honest man, he could have taken as much of this coin with him as he and his servants could have carried on his overland trip through Texas to the City of Mexico.

Totally differing from him on the leading questions of currency and tariff, and above all on the injurious consequences of his teachings in favor of secession, I do not think that the final influence of his energies, talents, and courage upon the public mind of his State and country will be beneficial. But nevertheless there was much in him to admire. His directness of purpose, his courage, his scorn and contempt for political trimmers, his generosity to the poor (for his purse was ever open to them), his industry, his iron will—these were excellent qualities, and to them he largely owed the great popularity he had with the people of Tennessee and his success in public life.

But there were some questions on which we had kindred sympathies. For the oppressed people of Ireland, for the struggling patriots of Cuba, for the vindication of the rights of American citizens in foreign lands, he had strongly pronounced opinions. And our sympathies were kindred in opposition to that greatest of modern humbugs, miscalled "civil-service reform." Senator HARRIS was too manly to pretend to favor the law while secretly endeavoring to have it violated, but he was openly opposed to this un-Democratic, anti-Republican system of life tenure in office holding. He was as much in favor of honesty and efficiency in the public service as the pretentious people who shout loudest for reform. He knew that—

> A man may cry Church! Church! at ev'ry word
> With no more piety than other people—
> A daw 's not reckoned a religious bird
> Because it keeps a-cawing from a steeple.

We live too near the great war in which he was so potent a factor and the party strife growing out of it to expect that all should do justice to his good qualities of head and heart. He was as little influenced by a personally revengeful feeling as any man of positive opinions I ever knew. He could hate what he believed to be political heresy and yet cherish kindly personal feelings toward those whom he knew held such views. In this respect he was more liberal in spirit than many of the leaders of his party or of his provincial supporters in the lowlands of middle and western Tennessee.

Senator HARRIS was not a man of education or culture as these terms are usually understood, nor was he an orator according to the generally accepted definition of that term. He was what neither education nor culture nor oratory can make—he was a tireless and fearless worker. He was not a scholar as

S. Doc. 343——8

implying knowledge of books, but in a larger sense he was not untaught. He had a marvelous knowledge of men and how to control them. His speeches were terse, vigorous, full of enthusiasm. They were practical, dealing in facts, never above the comprehension of the popular assemblies he addressed, and calculated to produce the effect which is both the purpose and result of true oratory—that of challenging attention and producing conviction.

In breadth of intellect I do not think he was equal to Jackson, White, Grundy, Bell, or Johnson, who preceded him in the Senate, but as a party organizer and leader he surpassed them all. As an organizer of campaigns he never had an equal in Tennessee, and often during the past ten years his party would have been badly beaten under the leadership of any other man. Tennessee has furnished more names that stand high on the national rôle of honor than any State save Virginia and Massachusetts. Not to mention Tennesseeans who, like Claiborne, of Louisiana; Sharkey, Yerger, and Cocke, of Mississippi; Gwin, of California; Tipton, of Indiana; Sevier, of Arkansas; Benton and Barton, of Missouri; Henry Watterson of Kentucky; Houston, of Texas, and Commodore M. F. Maury, who attained influence and celebrity, either local or national, in other States. Tennessee has given to the National Government a number of Presidents and Cabinet officers entirely out of proportion to its wealth and population.

We have furnished one Secretary of the Treasury, two Secretaries of War, one Attorney-General, and four Postmasters-General. To this House Tennessee has furnished two Speakers and to the Senate two presiding officers, one of whom was ISHAM G. HARRIS. Besides having had three Presidents, Tennessee has had two unsuccessful candidates for the Presidency, each of whom received the electoral votes of several

States. We have had two associate justices of the Supreme Court of the United States. In addition to this Tennessee has furnished many representatives to the diplomatic service. But of this brilliant galaxy few were equal in force of character and ability to the late Senator HARRIS. His political convictions in the most important period of his life were on trial in the midst of remorseless war, when thousands of his friends were going down before the iron tempest of battle. He should be judged by the times in which he lived. That he possessed many manly qualities none can deny.

" Let us pass him to the grave as we would have others pass ourselves, forgetting the frailties incident to our nature and which appear to be inseparably connected with our being."

ADDRESS OF MR. CLARKE OF NEW HAMPSHIRE

Mr. CLARKE of New Hampshire. Mr. Speaker, I did not know that arrangements had been made to-day to pay tribute to the memory of the distinguished statesman who most ably and honorably and for so long a time represented the great State of Tennessee in various high offices, or I should have prepared a suitable eulogy to his great fame and memory. But I can not, sir, allow the opportunity to pass without at least paying a word of tribute to the name and fame of Senator HARRIS. It was not my good fortune to know him closely as a companion or as a friend; but I thought I knew him as an able Senator and statesman, as a rugged, sturdy, honest man; and yet, as a member of the funeral party which accompanied the remains of the distinguished Senator to his late home at Memphis, when I approached the confines of the State which he had so honorably represented I soon learned my mistake—I then ascertained that I had but partially and imperfectly estimated the man.

When we reached the State of Tennessee, I found that his friends were legion and that they had all abandoned both business and pleasure and were present to pay their sad tribute to his fame, to his memory, and to his greatness. I remember the large concourse of people that met us at the capital of the State and the distinguished honor that all seemed anxious to pay to the statesman's memory. Rich and poor, high and low, everybody, seemed to be the friends of Senator HARRIS. They knew his work, they knew the great and valuable services that he had performed for them in his representative capacity in many ways, and they were there to add their last tribute to the great man who had been called beyond the borders that no eye can pierce. And when we reached his home, there was an impression made upon me that I shall never forget. I remember that distinguished gentlemen, representing all departments of business, all vocations in life, all professions, turned out as one man to meet the funeral party and to shed a tear at the loss of their neighbor and their friend. I remember, Mr. Speaker, as we entered that great church and took our places within the chancel the words of his pastor and that beautiful service of song, the words of which ring in my ears even to-day:

> Lay him low, lay him low;
> Under the clover, or under the snow,
> What cares he? He can not know.
> Lay him low, lay him low.

Mr. Speaker, we did lay him low; we accompanied his remains to that beautiful field of the dead, and I remember as the sun went down beyond those great shade trees that he had helped set out, and amid the scenes he loved so well, that we did not lay him into a cold, damp, stuffy grave, but rather in a repository that was literally smothered with flowers, brought there by people of all ages, all distinctions, all colors; and I said to myself, "Surely, Senator HARRIS, it is blessed to die under such circumstances as these, when all your neighbors and friends have come here, with one accord, to pay their sad tribute to your memory, and are saying, 'Well done, thou good and faithful servant; enter thou into the joy of thy Lord.'"

ADDRESS OF MR SIMS

Mr. SIMS. Mr. Speaker, the first public men that I have any recollection of hearing mentioned were Governor ISHAM G HARRIS, President Buchanan, Abraham Lincoln, and Jefferson Davis. I was only 8 years old, but remember distinctly hearing my father speak in the highest terms of Governor HARRIS, although my father was an intense Whig.

I went out to Camp Alger a few days ago, and it reminded me of the first gathering of volunteer soldiers that I ever saw, thirty-seven years ago, assembled at the call of Governor ISHAM G. HARRIS, of Tennessee. When those volunteers of 1861, those that were left of them, returned to their desolate and ruined homes in the spring of 1865, my childish heart prayed that the day might never come again in the history of this country when there would be a call for volunteers to go forth to fight other volunteers of our own blood and brotherhood; and, thank God, so far that prayer has been answered.

After so much has been said of the life and character of Senator HARRIS by those so much more able and better fitted to do justice to his fame and memory, I feel great delicacy in attempting to speak here to-day, for fear that I may rather detract from than add to the interest of the occasion.

Senator HARRIS'S early years were spent in the beautiful and intellectual little city of Paris, the county seat of Henry County, noted then, as at present, for its public men of national reputation. Such a home and surroundings were well calculated to develop the talents of the young and ambitious HARRIS. While his home was at Paris he was twice elected to represent that district on this floor. His beloved wife died there only a short while before the death of her illustrious husband.

On account of the long and intimate association of Senator HARRIS with the people of the Eighth district of Tennessee, I should feel that I had not discharged my full duty if I did not at this time and on this occasion give some expression of the esteem in which he was held by his old friends and associates.

Senator HARRIS was in public life almost continuously for over fifty years, and in all that time never suffered even a temporary defeat, while at times he had to and did overcome an adverse party and political majority. Of how few of our successful public men can the same be said? While courteous and affable, he was not that character of man known as a good electioneerer, a good hand shaker. He was rather blunt and plain in his manner and address, but always sincere and candid. He was a man of great moral and physical courage. He was not a political diplomat. He never sought to accomplish his purposes by scheming or machine methods. He spurned an attempt at indirection.

It was never charged against him that he belonged to any political ring or that he was in any sense a party boss. His was a most positive character, bordering on the dogmatic. He had enemies, as all such men have, but he was never revengeful. He never sought to popularize his views by other means than clear and forcible arguments, tersely stated. He used no circumlocution, no confusing platitudes. When he stated a proposition, no one, however simple or untutored, could possibly misunderstand him.

While there is perhaps no single great legislative enactment bearing his name, there was no man in the Senate during the last twenty years who had or exerted a greater influence in the national legislation of that period than Senator HARRIS. There was no man in the Senate of the United States during his long period of service whose word was more implicitly relied on. No one ever questioned his sincerity or honesty. It is useless to give details or circumstances to justify this statement, as no enemy personal or political, ever questioned his honor or integrity.

While Senator HARRIS was twice a member of this body, three times governor of Tennessee, and twenty years a Senator, all the details of his public career have been so fully stated by others who have gone before me that it is unnecessary that I should make further mention of them at this time. I suppose that if all his acts of usefulness during his long and eventful public life were stated in detail it would require volumes to contain them.

Senator HARRIS was endowed with a most remarkable memory. I will ask the indulgence of the House to relate an incident that goes to show how great a memory he possessed. In the campaign of 1876 Governor HARRIS and Gen. William B. Bate, now the honored senior Senator from Tennessee, were to deliver addresses at an old-fashioned Democratic rally and barbecue held in Linden, Tenn., then and now my home.

I was selected, together with Dr. S. A. McDonald, to go to Waynesboro, the county seat of Wayne County, 30 miles distant, and pilot Governor HARRIS through the country to Linden. Dr. McDonald and I were on horseback, while Governor HARRIS and his son were in a buggy. About halfway between Waynesboro and Linden, while riding some 200 yards in advance of the buggy, we saw a covey of birds by the side of the road.

Dr. McDonald alighted and picked up a stone, threw it into the covey, and killed two of the birds. We waited until his buggy came up and gave the birds to Governor HARRIS. We went on to within 8 miles of Linden, and stopped over at the home of Dr. McDonald for lunch and to feed and rest the horse the Governor was driving. The birds were at once dressed and cooked, and Govorner HARRIS ate them. Twenty years after this date, at the time Senator HARRIS was elected to the Senate for the fourth consecutive term, I was in Nashville and with Gen. M. H. Meeks, called on Senator HARRIS at his hotel to pay our respects and to congratulate him on his election without opposition.

I had not met him since that trip from Waynesboro to Linden. At the time I piloted him through the country as above stated I was very thin in flesh, but at the time I met him at his hotel I had become stout. When I presented myself, the Senator took me by the hand and looked me steadily in the face, as was his custom. I said to him that I was the young man "who, twenty years before, had piloted him from Waynesboro to Linden," and asked him if he remembered me. He replied "Oh, yes, I do; and I remember those birds that Dr. McDonald killed and that I ate for my dinner that day."

The incident had long passed out of my mind, but the Senator remembered it quite well. He then gave every incident and detail of his visit to Linden, and what occurred after he arrived, and the names of old friends he met while there, and related all that took place on the day of the barbecue, with much more circumstantial detail than I could have possibly done.

Only a short time before his death I heard him go over the details of court trials in which he had been engaged that had taken place more than fifty years before, giving all the minute particulars as though they had occurred only the day before.

For many years before he died he was regarded by the whole people of Tennessee with the warmest feelings of affection. He was lovingly called "the old Senator." When "the old Senator" made a promise, no one ever entertained the slightest doubt but that he would most faithfully keep it.

No public man has passed from this life within the last fifty years who was so universally mourned throughout the State of Tennessee as was Senator HARRIS. Expressions of heartfelt and sincere grief knew no party lines. At an informal meeting which took place at the Ebbitt House, in this city, on the night after his death, was gathered every Tennessean in the national capital to give fitting expression as to the great loss our beloved State had sustained in his death.

In that meeting were men of all shades of political opinion. In that meeting were men gathered together from the highest to the lowest walks of life. The gray-haired statesman of wide national reputation sat beside the humblest Department employee, all drawn together by a common sorrow; all grieving over the loss of a loved and cherished friend. No one could tell who was republican or Democrat in that assembly, but anyone could easily see that all were sincere mourners. Such distinguished Republicans as Hon. A. H. Pettibone, Hon. W. P. Brownlow, Gen. George H. Maney, and many others were present and took conspicuous part in the proceedings, all evincing a genuine and unaffected sorrow.

No man that ever lived had truer friends than Senator HARRIS, and no man ever lived who was more faithful and devoted to his friends than was Senator HARRIS.

Though dead, yet does he live. His life and teachings are to-day exerting a great and lasting beneficial influence over the minds of our young people. He has left us an example that we will do well to imitate. His life and accomplishments are a hope and a comfort to those worthy and ambitious youths of our land who are hampered and cramped by poverty.

He was in the most literal sense a self-made man. Beginning life without money or influential friends at the tender age of 14 years, by his own unaided efforts he won the highest positions within the gift of the people. He is a conspicuous example of what can be accomplished in this goodly land of ours by untiring effort and perseverance. His life will be a beacon light to worthy thousands who are now struggling against the cold and chilly waves of adversity and poverty.

Mr. Speaker, Senator HARRIS did not live in vain, and he has not died in vain. Full of years and honors, he sleeps the sleep of the just.

ADDRESS OF MR. DE ARMOND

Mr. DE ARMOND. Mr. Speaker, I do not know that the deaths in the present Congress have been more numerous than the average in preceding Congresses; but it has seemed to me that the stricken ones were unusually prominent. Out of this House went that man of long service and great usefulness, William Steele Holman. From the Senate were taken Senator Earle, of South Carolina (a new man in the body, but eminent in his State), two great Senators from the State of Mississippi, and the great veteran Senator from the State of Tennessee. In these notable deaths our attention has been directed pointedly to the fact that a number of great men of the older period, of the generation to which but few now living belong, have passed from us lately; and scarcely can we hope that the present and the oncoming generation will be equal to the task of filling as well as they filled the places which they vacated.

It is not much that I can add to what has been said in sketching the career and outlining the salient points of the character of the distinguished Senator from Tennessee. It has been said very truthfully that he was one of the foremost men of his day and generation—gifted with great ability, a man of superb courage, a man honest and direct in all his methods. Through a long period in the service of his State and his country, his triumphs have been such as but few men reach and scarcely any can rival.

At first blush it might seem to us that, starting as he started, poor and obscure, is a disadvantage in the great race of life. To the comparatively weak, the timid and the fearful especially, poverty and the lack of influential family do indeed amount to great hindrances—hindrances that often make miscarriage and shipwreck of all the voyage of life. But, however it may be in other countries, it is true, I think, in this, that a considerable portion of the men really strong by nature are made stronger by early contact with poverty and early experience of privation. We often look upon the careers of our great men in retrospect and say to ourselves that they would have been much greater, that their achievements would have been more marked and their success more signal if they had started in life with better advantages; if their early opportunities had been superior to what they were; if family influence had given them aid which they were denied.

I believe, however, that in this country such an idea involves a superficial and incorrect view of the possibilities of life and the achievements of our great men. In a country like this, where the people do their own governing—where the people are the great power, the source of all power, and where those who fairly attain high position and honestly retain it long must be intrenched in the confidence and support of the people—it seems to me nothing so well fits a man for an illustrious career, nothing so securely binds him to the interests of the great masses of the people as the hard but valuable experiences in youth of a life of penury, of toil, of sacrifice.

This country can attain its high destiny—the people of this country can be measurably prosperous and happy—only when those who administer the laws, those who are clothed with great power, capable of great things good or bad, are true to the interests of the masses. Steadfast fidelity to the public interests generally can be found in large measure only with those who partake of the feelings and sentiments and experiences—who enter experimentally into the lives—of the great masses of the people. Those who have been brought up in affluence, those whose early opportunities were great, those who have had the pathway of life made smooth and easy for them from beginning to end—they can not, from the very nature of things, enter into the lives, appreciate the motives, understand the difficulties, estimate properly the rights and the duties of that stern, that noble citizenship which belongs to the common people of our great Republic.

With very few exceptions—there are some notable ones—the men who have made illustrious the history of this country, who have been benefactors of human kind in their age and generation, who laid the foundations of this Republic and builded the nation, who sustained it in times of trial and who will sustain it in all the years to come, they have been and are those who came from the plain level of the people—the men with the experiences which are common to the masses, and therefore with the sympathies which must reside in those who represent properly, and who only can thus represent, the great body of American citizenship.

This man was peculiarly strong in that respect. His early struggles with poverty, his early privations, his early triumphs over difficulties which assail so many in a country like ours, marked him and fitted him for the great career which he rounded grandly. Without high ability, without superb courage, without unshaken honesty, without fidelity to friend and candor in dealing with the foe he never could have been as great as he was; and perhaps he never could have developed in high degree any of the great, the inestimable, the noble qualities which he exhibited if he had not had that stern, hard discipline in youth and early manhood in which such qualities are developed if the germ of them exist at all.

But a few years ago, Mr. Speaker, when the great party to which the departed Senator belonged was considering, away back in the school districts, in the small conventions and the chance assemblages of the masses of its people, questions of vital party and national ·importance; when a great question was brought up within the lines of the Democracy to which he was devoted as to whether the few or the many should control within the party; as to what should be declared as the party creed; as to who should be in command and who, for the good of the party, should be retired—I recollect that then he was one of four great Senators, men of influence and might in the party, men of influence and might in the country, who were instrumental in assembling, in an unofficial way, a large number of representatives of the party in his well-loved city of Memphis, to consider, quietly and as American citizens, what ought to be done, what the needs of the party and the country were in the crisis through which we then were passing.

To Senator HARRIS, Senator George, Senator Turpie, and Senator Jones of Arkansas—they are the four whom I remember particularly and preeminently—from the standpoint of those who think as I think and who try to act as I try to act with regard to these great public questions, a world of gratitude is due. Then there took form in the great party of which Senator HARRIS was an exemplar and a leader that which was in the minds of the masses. The movement then inaugurated and put fairly upon its feet gathered strength and force until a year later the efforts of those who thought as he thought were crowned with success, and the representatives of the party, meeting in national convention, declared at Chicago what the true party creed was, what the true party creed should be.

Very much indeed did this dead Senator add to the reputation of the State, already great, which he honored and which honored him. High, no doubt, will he· rank in all time to come among the great men of that great State. High will he rank as long as the annals of Congress are read or known among the great men of this nation. He possessed in marked degree qualities which it has sometimes seemed to me are not too common not too generally found in public men. He was thoroughly devoted to any cause in which he was enlisted. He was thoroughly open and direct in his methods, and his position, once taken, was held with Spartan tenacity. He may have seemed impetuous in advocacy, as has been remarked here this afternoon; he may have seemed impetuous in action, but it was the impetuosity of courage and conviction.

The subject considered, the conclusion reached, the die cast, he may have appeared impetuous in execution. Nothing remained but to make known the decision and to act upon the lines deliberately chosen. In action there is no time for consideration of whether there should be action. When the charge is sounded there is no time for considering whether it should have been sounded. Senator HARRIS distinctively recognized this, as every great man in history has recognized it, and acted upon it. Careful and cautious in reaching his conclusions, thorough in his investigations, his conclusions once reached, his determination once arrived at, the time for action once at hand, he was impetuous in the charge—there was no halting and no hesitancy about his course. He struck home, struck quick, and struck hard. It was this quality, among others which he possessed in a high degree, that made him the conspicuous figure that he was and that he will remain in the history of our country.

Beautiful and feeling tributes have been paid to his memory by those who knew him personally far better than I did. Distinguished men from his own State have delighted to praise him by telling the truth about him. Distinguished men throughout the land, while they may not have known him so well, delight also to join, though far distant they may be, with their tribute. And the great mass of the people the country over, forgetting whatever faults he may have had—and all men have faults—recognized that his virtues triumphed over his faults and in their splendid glow obscured them almost entirely from view.

Among all the great men of the land, Tennessee's venerable Senator ever will stand as one of the most able, most courageous, most useful. Such a standing few men attain. Such a standing reflects at once honor upon the man who attains it; honor upon those connected with him by blood, by position, by association; honor upon the community which honors him, and which he in turn honors. Such a man, with such standing, was ISHAM G. HARRIS.

S. Doc. 343——9

ADDRESS OF MR. GAINES.

Mr. GAINES. Mr. Speaker, Senator HARRIS was in public life many years before I was born. I was not privileged to be socially intimate with him for the reason that his home was in the distant end of the State; but from my earliest childhood my father taught me to love and respect him, and as I grew to manhood I learned to look up to him as a leader, a patriot, and a statesman worthy the exalted love of a great people. I have frequently asked myself "Why do the people love this man so devotedly?" and I found its solution when I came to know him and his works better. It was because he never abused their confidence.

No man has ever lived to say that ISHAM G. HARRIS deceived him. I have wondered also why it was that his political foes held him in such high esteem, and I have concluded that it was because they always knew where to find him and he never struck below the belt. He was a man of magnificent courage, physically and morally. Never in his long and splendid public life did he palter with truth or hesitate between two opinions. He dared to be right. What lofty courage it sometimes requires! He never betrayed a trust, and he made candor the cardinal principle of his life.

Senator HARRIS was stricken with his fatal illness shortly after I entered upon my duties at this capital, and I was denied much of his wise counsel which I had so much depended upon to equip me for duty here; but as a Tennessean and one of his constituents and disciples I am joint heir to a rich heritage of benefit that flowed out of his great and eventful life. His mind retained its vigor until the last. When the hand of death was upon him and he awaited with calm fortitude the dire event, I called upon him and found him greatly interested in the four-days adjournment question then pending, and with wonderful precision and almost supernatural clearness he laid down the principles involved, which I afterwards found the law books verified. He had not investigated the books; it was intuitive, evolved out of his own innate wisdom.

Mr. Speaker, when this great spirit had winged its flight to other spheres, we took up the wasted tenement it had so long occupied and bore it lovingly to Tennessee, where his people might do it honor, and the multitudes of people, regardless of politics, creed, or race, who crowded past his bier bore eloquent though tearful testimonial to the universality of that love which they all bore him. On that occasion, when the best men of Tennessee were assembled to pay tribute to his memory, Col. John J. Vertrees, of Nashville, presented resolutions, which I ask to have printed here, together with the remarks he made, and I offer them in lieu of further remarks myself. They pay masterful tribute to the memory and deeds of a great man, and I ask that they be printed here that they may be perpetuated in the forum he so long honored.

A ADDRESS OF MR. CARMACK

Mr. CARMACK. Mr. Speaker, it was the profound remark of a wise old Mohammedan caliph that men are more like the times they live in than they are like their fathers. Mind and character are cast in the mold of environment; they take form and color from their surroundings, they are fashioned to the hour by the plastic hand of circumstance. Types of character come and go with the varying phases of social, economic, and political conditions, of national growth or decay. Times change and men change with them. The rough-hewn characters who lay the foundations of empire in the midst of pains and perils are but feebly stamped upon the lineaments of a softer age. We are not born of the dead past, but are children of the living hour. Upon its Procrustean bed the tyrannical present fits each generation to its own whim or need.

IsHAM G. HARRIS was a survival of a type which has passed or is fast passing with the conditions that gave it birth—the old frontier or pioneer type. He was born in the early years of the century, when Tennessee was but young in the Union, when the smell of the wilderness yet lingered in the air of its new-born civilization, when the character of the age drew its sap and vigor from the forest mold. He possessed all the essential qualities of the hardy and heroic statesmen-warriors who on the Watauga and the Cumberland made a clearing for civilization and free government. He was of the mold and fiber of Andrew Jackson; a character of massive simplicity, of heroic force and clearness; fearless, resolute, masterful, and imperious, he was born to lead, and, by the sheer force of his personality, to rule.

The composition of his nature was not complex or intricate—

its elements were few and simple. To know him at all was to know him well. Long years of close and intimate association only strengthened and deepened the earlier impressions. You were never startled or surprised by the revelation of new and unexpected traits, except that the softer and gentler side of his character was not kept on public exhibition. In his many acts of kindness and generosity, indeed, his left hand was hardly suffered to know what his right hand did. Otherwise all his traits and qualities were stripped to every eye.

His intellect was not subtle or ingenious, but robust, vigorous, direct, guided always by unfailing common sense. His judgment was wonderfully swift and wonderfully true. He was not widely or deeply read—though he knew accurately the political history of his own country—but he knew men, and he understood the springs of human action.

His long public career, unbroken by a single defeat, is worthy of study, for it is stored with lessons to the rising generation, in which may be learned the secret of failure or success. He lived a life full of stormy conflicts, in which were given many a hard and bitter blow—blows which left behind them lasting enmities and unforgiving animosities. Yet from the first to the last of his long career victory clung to his standard, and amid all the great and rapid political changes of his time popular confidence never wavered from the man who adhered with stubborn, defiant, combative tenacity to his earliest creed.

Many a man his equal in intellect and in many other qualities of leadership would have gone down in any one of the many storms through which he passed triumphantly and with honor. His success was a triumph not so much of intellect as of character. The people had marked him as a man worthy of confidence, and he justified their faith, not by seeking to find and follow the popular opinion, but to instruct and guide it. He dealt with perfect candor both with individuals and the public. He was, I believe, the most truthful man I have ever known. His statements of fact were never colored or warped from the line of accuracy by prejudice or self-interest.

Perhaps the highest tribute that could be paid him is to be found in the negative fact that, though he lived for years under the full blaze of a passionate and hostile criticism, no accusation tainting his honor has ever adhered to his fame. No charge of double-dealing, of deception, or even of a lack of full and perfect candor was ever laid at his door. His bitterest foes have been forced to admit that Isham G. Harris was a man to be trusted when he had given his word.

Such qualities as these won and retained for him throughout all his stormy life the unshaken confidence of the people. He had few of the arts of a popular politician. His manner was lacking in warmth and cordiality, and, except to those who knew him well, he often seemed distant and reserved. With a marvelous memory for fact and incident, he had a poor memory for names and faces, and he never affected to remember a face he had forgotten.

His enemies, who could not or would not understand his success, attributed it in large measure to his matchless skill in the management of a well-organized machine. Yet in truth no man ever profited less by such methods. His methods were perfectly open, straightforward, and direct. He made no promises. He sought no alliances. He wrote few letters and made few suggestions as to the management of his own political affairs. He went straight to the people and appealed to them from the hustings, and there he won all his battles.

No man in Tennessee was ever more powerful or effective as a public speaker, and he was preeminently so in joint discussion, where all the latent power and fire of his nature were stirred by the presence of a strong antagonist. In the days when the Whig and Democratic parties in Tennessee possessed an unusual array of brilliant orators, ISHAM G. HARRIS was the peer of the best. He met in joint debate such masters of political controversy as Neil S. Brown, Robert Hatton, John Netherland, and others, and no antagonist ever bore away from him the prize of combat. He was not a phrase maker or a rhetorician, but he possessed the faculty of sinewy, terse, incisive speech, with intense earnestness of manner, an impressive delivery, and a gift of plain and logical presentation. His manner of public speaking may be described as argument, warm and glowing with earnestness and passion.

In the discharge of public duty he was rigidly conscientious. He loved to do things well—not brilliantly or with splendid dramatic effect, but well. It was not enough for him to gain the approval of his countrymen. His conduct and the results were subjected to the merciless analysis of his own judgment and scrupulously tested by his own estimate of the scope and measure of his duty.

It would not be true to say that he took no thought of his own fame; but no man ever made less effort to gain a factitious popularity. No man ever did less purely to win public approval. He did not delight in the applause of the moment. He valued only that solidly built esteem formed to endure the impartial criticism of the future and against which the pitiless years may beat in vain.

He trusted the people as implicitly as they trusted him; he trusted not only their good intentions but their intelligence and capacity for self-government. Believing, with never a shadow of doubt, in the truth and righteousness of his own principles, he was never apprehensive as to his own political fortunes. But even to the people he never stooped his high, imperial crest.

He never wheedled them or cringed to or flattered them. His kingly manhood stood erect in the pride and dignity of its character, and he faced the people confidently and without fear. It was a confidence both in himself and in them.

He was never troubled with doubts. His opinions once formed were never clouded by any vague misgivings. His beliefs and his purposes were always as clear as the noonday to his own mind. He never groped in the fog or stumbled in the dark. He knew his way and walked with confidence.

In the course of his long and eventful career the fiber of his character was many times put to the sternest trial. When the war of secession began, he was serving his second term as governor of Tennessee. He was a thoroughgoing secessionist. He believed in secession, both as a constitutional doctrine and as a practical remedy. He believed that it was impossible for the Union to endure and the institutions of the South to be preserved, and with characteristic courage he accepted the inevitable. Tennessee was slow to yield to the secession movement, and Senator HARRIS's enemies have often said that he dragged it out of the Union against its will. Certain it is that the tremendous force of his personality was a powerful factor in bringing the State under the banner of the Confederacy.

As governor of Tennessee his resourcefulness, his marvelous energy, his intuitive judgment and decision of character, his thorough knowledge of men, his genius for administration, made him the greatest war governor of the South. In spite of the fact that his capital was in the hands of the enemy and that a large part of his State was loyal to the Union, he gave to the Confederacy 100,000 soldiers thoroughly organized and equipped. It had been his purpose upon the expiration of his term as governor to take command in the field; but because his successor could not be inaugurated owing to the capital being in the hands of his enemy, he served as governor to the end of the war. He was, however, with the army of Tennessee from the time of the fall of Nashville, rendering gallant and conspicuous service. He was volunteer aid on the staff of Gen. Albert Sidney Johnston at the battle of Shiloh, and in the thick of all that bloody fray. He rallied in person a Tennessee regiment which was retreating in disorder and led it back to the position from which it had been driven. He was by the side of General Johnston when fatally wounded, and bore him from the field.

The end of the war found him broken in fortune, an exile from his country, the proscribed representative of a ruined cause. But he returned to face the new duties, problems, and responsibilities of the hour, and he faced them with courage and practical wisdom. It was not in his nature to repine. He cherished no illusions as to the results of the war. He saw what had been irretrievably lost and what might yet be saved from the wreck and ruin. He turned from the dead past with sorrow and faced the future with high resolve. His dearest hopes had been entwined with the fallen Confederacy; but he knew that the cause he loved had died on the field of battle and he did not withhold his beloved from the grave. Thenceforth the destiny of his people was to be cast with the Union, and under its flag and law its future must redeem its past. To the Union, therefore, sincerely and ungrudgingly, he gave his renewed allegiance.

He reentered public life as a candidate in the Presidential election of 1876. His name was in that year presented to the Democratic convention as one of the electoral candidates for the State at large. There developed in the convention an unexpected opposition to his candidacy. There was still some prejudice against him among the "Old Line Whigs." There were those who feared that his conspicuous activity in the secession

movement would alienate a considerable body of Union Demo
crats and there were the usual number of pusillanimous spirits
who always visit the blame of their misfortunes upon the leader
of the unsuccessful cause

All these sentiments found voice in the convention. He was
nominated in spite of this opposition but, stung to the quick,
he appeared before the convention and in a speech full of patriotic fire declined to allow his name to be the cause of discord
in the ranks of his party. All opposition was swept away in
the enthusiasm which his speech evoked, and in spite of his
declination the convention again selected him by an almost
unanimous vote. He adhered, however, to his decision and
announced that he would canvass the State on his own responsibility. So effective were the series of speeches which he
delivered in that memorable campaign that by the time the legislature assembled there was not an opponent to dispute his
election to the Senate.

Upon his subsequent career I need not dwell. It is enough
to say that during all the years of his service in the Senate he
held fast to his fundamental conception of Democracy a strict
construction of the Constitution. To that doctrine, as to the
Ark of the Covenant, he fixed his faith and hope.

During all these years he was the acknowledged leader of the
Tennessee Democracy, infallible in council and invincible in the
field. The growing infirmities of age never dimmed his mind,
weakened his intellectual energies, or abated his zeal for the
principles he loved.

In the great battle of 1896, though weakened by disease, his
interest in the campaign burned with unwonted energy and
power. Perhaps it was because he realized, as I know he did,
that amid the tumults of the next Presidential contest, the
"thunder of the captains and the shouting," his voice would

not be heard. He felt, like Ossian, that this was the "last of his fields." He determined to give the last remnant of his strength to liberty and the people.

> Charge once more, and then be dumb;
> Let the victors when they come,
> When the forts of folly fall,
> Find thy body by the wall.

His last days were characteristic of the man. He had known for weeks that death was upon him. He accepted it serenely and without a murmur. It is natural for men when the hope of life has passed or is passing away to seek consolation in the sympathy of those about them, to touch their hearts to pity by allusions to the dread event, and find a wretched comfort in the sorrow of their loved ones. Not so with him. He trod the wine press alone. For long weeks and months he looked steadily in the face of the king of terrors, and his own stout heart, which had sustained him through life, sustained him in death. Calmly, silently, and heroically he awaited the "inevitable hour."

A character both unique and great has passed. His conquering spirit, his iron will, his brave and true and generous heart, will be with us no more amid the scenes of this mortal life. In the soil of his own beloved State his ashes have been laid to rest, and sorrow's tears will keep green his grave, while love and honor will sentinel the hallowed spot where he sleeps his last, long sleep. We may not hope to see another who can draw his bow or wield his sword, for "he was a man, take him for all in all; we shall not look upon his like again."

ADDRESS OF MR. HARTMAN.

Mr. HARTMAN Mr. Speaker, once again has the House of Representatives been called upon to pay the tribute of its respect to one of the distinguished servants of the Republic. Senator ISHAM G. HARRIS, whose memory we revere and whose death we sincerely regret, was one of the strong, original, and patriotic characters of the present generation.

But few men in the history of the Republic have been called upon to fill so many and varied places of responsibility as he. In no place of public trust which was assigned to him was there ever the suggestion of the failure of the full performance of duty. In the great and momentous conflict of 1861 to 1865 he took his place where his conscience told him his duty lay, and while I, like many others, am entirely convinced that his decision was wrong, yet no one who knew him will ever question the sincerity of his belief or the honesty of his purpose. When the great strife was over and the disaffections and disagreements of North and South were in process of reconciliation, he contributed by his counsel and by his example very greatly to the accomplishment of the desired result.

In all of his legislative career those who knew him best, whether agreeing with him politically or opposing him, were glad to attribute to his every act the highest and purest motives which control public men. One trait of his character which stood out most prominent was his positive, aggressive, firm, and courageous stand upon all questions of public moment which had received long and serious investigation at his hands. At times some of his associates were tempted to become annoyed at his very abrupt and positive way of giving utterance to his feelings, but a more mature knowledge of his character has generally resulted in the conviction among his associates that whatever words he uttered or whatever act he performed were inspired by the loftiest and most patriotic of purposes.

Numerous conversations with many of his colleagues in the Senate have convinced me that among his associates he easily took rank as the leader of that body in questions of parliamentary procedure and practice. His speeches upon the great money question, the question of the tariff, and other subjects of public concern rank among the best delivered in either body of Congress. The influence of his life and character upon the rising generations of the Republic has been and will continue to be most beneficial.

Through all his long career of public service, extending from a time prior to the late war up to the day of his death, his reputation for integrity, for patriotism, for courage has never been doubted.

These are the three most essential and most desirable traits of character to be possessed by a public man. It is fitting, then, that the Congress of the United States should, by the adoption of the resolution presented, pay this their last tribute of respect to the memory of this distinguished man.

ADDRESS OF MR. SELZER

Mr. SELZER: Mr. Speaker, we meet to-day to pay a fitting and a deserved tribute to the memory of the Hon. ISHAM G. HARRIS, late a Senator from the State of Tennessee. He was a great man in many respects. He was an honest man, a true man, and a fearless man. He had a most remarkable and eventful career. I knew him and admired him for his great and sterling qualities of head and heart. He was one of the plain people. He stood for the rights of man, he battled for the masses, and he championed the cause of equal rights and equal opportunities for all. For over half a century he was an heroic and a prominent figure in the life of the Republic.

The story of his life has been eloquently and truthfully told here to-day by those who knew him best and loved him most. That story is a book that every youth in all the land should read. The history of the life of Senator HARRIS will be an incentive and a bright star of hope to every boy and every man struggling with poverty, with adversity, and with adverse circumstances. He demonstrated that success is toil, hard work and struggle; that if you want to progress you must plod on and on.

Senator HARRIS was a man of few words, but those words were always eloquent, sincere, direct, and they spoke and meant volumes. He always told the truth; he did not believe words were made to conceal thoughts. He had no cant, no chicanery, no hypocrisy; he loved truth for the sake of truth; he loved justice for the sake of justice. He was no pretender; he never dissembled; he cared naught for expediency. He was a man of noble impulses, with a high sense of honor and an unblemished character. He was not always right, he made mistakes in human ways like other human beings, but they were the mistakes of the head and not of the heart; his heart was always true, and he always did his duty as he saw it; he never flinched. He had few principles, few rules of life, few maxims, but those he had he adhered to with bulldog tenacity.

He did not believe in compromises. He did not believe in halfway measures. With him a thing was either right or wrong. He tested every proposition in the crucible of experience, of truth, and of justice. If it could not stand the test, he had no use for it; he was then open and aboveboard against it. He always had the courage of his convictions. No one ever doubted where he stood on any question.

He was Tennessee's grand old man for the last two decades of his life. He was born on her soil, and lived within her confines nearly all his life. He was one of her greatest sons and the product of her own free institutions. He loved his State, and his State loved him. He stood by her people, and they always stood by him. For years he was their popular idol, and during his long and stormy political career he never met with a political defeat when he submitted his cause to them and appealed to the people of his own State. The people of Tennessee knew him, they loved him, they revered him, and they honored him as they have few men in the history of that grand old Commonwealth. He deserved it all. He never betrayed their confidence. He was true to every trust confided to him.

He was a sterling Democrat, a disciple of Thomas Jefferson and a follower of Andrew Jackson. He lived in early life in their day. He knew their principles, and at all times he struggled for them and fought for them most tenaciously. He could not surrender principle. He loved the Constitution; he believed in a strict construction of it and in the reserved rights of the sovereign States. He believed in a government of the people, and he believed the people could be trusted and were capable of self-government.

He was a robust man, of great physical endurance and capable of great mental exertion. He was a busy man, a hard-working man. His life work is a great monument, more enduring than marble and brass of human effort, human endeavor, and human accomplishment. He exhausted every subject he considered. He went to the bottom of every proposition, and by eternal and fundamental principles determined whether it was right or wrong. He took nothing for granted—he proved all things.

He was a self-made man. He graduated from no college, but from the university of hard work and experience. He knew books and he read books, but he knew men and read men better. He was at home in nature, and he was a past master in human nature. He understood the motives, the hopes and the fears, the passions and the prejudices of men. He was not narrow-minded, not bigoted; he was broad, liberal, and charitable.

He thought for himself. He had opinions of his own. He was a direct, a positive man.

He had enemies, he made enemies; but for every enemy he made by reason of his inflexible character and his positive assertion of opinion he made a thousand friends. What forceful, positive man ever lived without enemies? A man without an enemy is a man without an opinion, and generally without a friend.

He lived long before the great conflict of States and long after. He was always an active man, a go-ahead kind of a man, and during all his long career he was a part of the life and history of his country. He made history. He met Napoleon's test—he did something.

He was born on the 10th day of February, 1818; nearly eighty years afterwards he died in harness, a Senator in Congress from his native State. He died in the capital city of his country on the 8th day of July, 1897. During all those years what a busy life was his!

The story of his struggles and triumphs, his reverses and successes, his poverty and his progress, his joys and sorrows, his trials and troubles, is one of the most interesting and instructive in biographical literature. It has been well told here to-day by many gentlemen more fluently and more eloquently than I can do. His life was a busy one, an exciting one, replete with incidents that read like a romance.

At the early age of 14 a clerk in a country store, at 21 a merchant doing business for himself, a few years later a lawyer with a good practice. Then a member of his State legislature, then a member of the House of Representatives, then twice governor of his State, then the war and the days that tried men's souls. In 1877 he was elected to the United States Senate, where he remained the balance of his life. It would take volumes to tell what he saw, what he did, and what he knew. What wonders have been accomplished during the fourscore years he lived! What a marvelous story of growth, of progress, of development, of expansion, of invention, of social evolution and commercial revolution! In all the history of the world there is nothing like it, nothing to equal it. Senator HARRIS lived and was a part of all this. He grew with events. He kept abreast of the times. He never lagged behind. He was always a leader.

His career in the Senate of the United States is remarkable alike for length of service and for duty well performed. He was a good debater and one of the best parliamentarians that ever lived. For many years he was the Democratic leader in that branch of the National Legislature. In the great duties which devolved on him he was zealous, patient and untiring. He was an indefatigable worker, and had the faculty of accomplishing a great deal in a short time. He was seldom absent, never neglected a duty, and his name is recorded on nearly every roll call. He realized his responsibility, and brought forth all his powers to intelligently and faithfully carry out his mission. No State ever had a more zealous and a more conscientious representative. All his life he stood for true Democracy, but in the Senate he had a mighty field to demonstrate the principles of Jefferson, Monroe, and Jackson and display his varied talents and profound knowledge.

He is dead and gone, but the great work he did lives in a thousand acts and volumes of Congress. That incomparable work is his enduring monument, and will live as long as the language in which it is indelibly written. He will live, too, in the memory of thousands and thousands whom he helped and befriended in innumerable ways. His life was a running chapter of kind and loving deeds. He knew a good deed lives and a kind act never dies.

He lived to a ripe old age. He died in the fullness of time—after his course was run, after he reached the goal. Looking back over the long vista of his eventful and exciting life, he had few regrets. His last moments were calm and placid. Surrounded by his friends and his loved ones, this grand old man yielded back the life and quietly and peacefully was gathered to his fathers.

In his death a nation mourned, and the State that gave him birth and all his honors put on the garb of sorrow. Her first and foremost citizen was no more.

This is my tribute, the tribute of New York, to the great and noble dead of Tennessee.

This is my tribute, poorly expressed, for human words after all but poorly express the feelings and the sentiments of the human heart. This, then, is my tribute to the memory of ISHAM G. HARRIS, toiler and lawyer, soldier and statesman, friend and humanitarian, and above all and beyond all a true, a noble, and an honest man, upon whose like we shall not look again.

Appendix

MEMORIAL EXERCISES.

Mr. W. J. Crawford, permanent chairman of the committee on arrangements and temporary chairman of the great meeting of the people at the Auditorium said:

LADIES AND GENTLEMEN: In behalf of the committee charged with the preparation of a memorial service befitting the dignity and character of the late Senator HARRIS, I take the liberty of calling this assemblage to order, and find pleasure in presenting the presiding officer on this occasion in the person of a man who is known, honored, and beloved throughout this country.

When in early manhood he served his country in a humble capacity in a foreign clime, and still later, when he by his peerless courage and indomitable will won the hearts of his command as well as the stars of a major-general, and subsequently, when full of years and full of honors, broadened and dignified with a ripe experience, he guided the helm of state and represented the Commonwealth in the Senate of the United States, he was and always has been prominent and preeminent by reason of the fidelity, courage, and integrity with which he served his cause and his people. When the people of this State and this country assemble to attest their respect for the memory and services of Senator HARRIS, it is eminently proper that he who for many years shared his burdens and his battles should preside over the ceremonies, and it is especially appropriate on an occasion such as this that the people should be given an opportunity to delicately express their high appreciation of one who has always served them with modesty, with manliness, and with ability—your senior Senator, Gen. William B. Bate.

Senator Bate, in assuming the chair, said:

Having been invited to preside over this memorial meeting,

and as others have been designated to deliver addresses suitable
to the occasion, it is not expected of me to present other than a
few words by way of introduction to that which is to follow.

Descending from a pioneer parentage, ISHAM GREEN HARRIS
was born in that beautiful and romantic part of Tennessee
where the waters of Elk River flow under the spurs of the Cumberland Mountains, which overlook the picturesque and produc-
tive valleys of Franklin County.

By birth, by early training, by education and development, he
was essentially, and all in all, a Tennesseean—and as the bud
unfolded into the blossom of practical life under the genial and
inspiring influences of that day which so splendidly developed
Tennessee and Tennesseeans, his natural attributes and tenden-
cies strengthened and matured into ripe manhood and clung to
him through his long and eventful career and, now that he is
gone, leave a resplendent memory.

Possessed of strong natural ability that was eminently practical, and backed by a will power and energy and an ambition
that had a spur within, ISHAM G. HARRIS began the battle of
life.

The time in which he lived afforded rare opportunities for
men of metal and merit to push to the front and gain distinction, and he readily and rightly availed himself of it. But to
follow his career would be to go through a large part of the
history of Tennessee during the last half century, and the time
allotted to introductory remarks will not allow it.

The chief and culminating point in his history, and that
which most attracted the public gaze, was the course he took at
the outbreak of the war, while he was governor of Tennessee.
The time, the occasion, and the office he held gave him such
opportunities as have rarely fallen to the lot of man. They
opened the way for service to his country in a great crisis, and
he gave it courageously, faithfully, and acceptably.

The keynote which he struck at the outset of hostilities when
called upon, as the governor of Tennessee, by President Lincoln
for men and means to use against the South was such a prompt,
laconic, and emphatic denial that it not only found favorable

response in Tennessee, but was applauded to the echo throughout the South.

The war being upon us, and the State of Tennessee having formally seceded from the Union, Governor HARRIS, as governor, mustered in and organized more than a hundred thousand soldiers for the Confederate service. Hence he is known to history as one of the "war governors."

Without going into detail it is sufficient to state that from the first reveille to the last tattoo in Confederate camps Governor HARRIS was an active factor in our great unequal contest.

Being by nature, as he was by profession a Democrat in its broadest and most liberal sense, he was easily a favorite with his people and was one of the leaders who was rarely if ever out of touch with them. Hence it was an easy matter for him to be elected to anything within their gift.

Since peace came unto us he was four times elected to the United States Senate from Tennessee. The State has honored him and he has honored the State. The Senate likewise honored him by electing him President pro tempore of the Senate, and he thus became its presiding officer in the absence of the Vice-President; and in this, as in other official places held by him, he became master of the situation and brought credit alike to himself and the office he held.

In no part of his life was Senator HARRIS ever a drone in the human hive, but an active participant in its make-up and management.

As an actor on the stage of life he played a leading part, and when the curtain fell at the close of the last act in the drama it but removed the actor from sight, leaving fresh and pleasant memories of his sayings and the impress of his doings upon those who saw and heard him.

But "Thy scythe and glass, O Time, are not the emblems of thy gentler power," for even "the Old Guard" must surrender to thy inexorable demands. Senator HARRIS, one of the last of the Old Guards—and they are getting scarce now—stood for twenty years in the Senate a sentinel to guard the Constitution of our country. But this faithful old sentinel has been called by the decree of fate from his post of duty, and his mother, Tennessee, has put him to rest in her bosom within the sacred precincts of your own Elmwood.

It is well—

> And if through patient toil we reach the land
>   Where tired feet, with sandals loose, may rest,
> Where we shall clearly see and understand,
>   I think that we will say, "God knew the best."

When Senator Bate had concluded his brief speech he asked the audience to rise, and then called upon the Rev. Dr. N. M. Woods, pastor of the Second Presbyterian Church, who offered prayer.

The invocation was impressive, asking the blessings of Heaven upon the exercises and praying God that the good lessons to be learned from the life of Senator HARRIS might be impressed upon all present.

Governor Taylor made a graceful speech as the representative of the State of Tennessee.

Professor Arnold's orchestra rendered a selection when Senator Turpie had concluded. The governor of Tennessee, Hon. Robert L. Taylor, was the next speaker, and Senator Bate introduced him as the representative of the State upon the occasion when citizens of the State would honor the dead who, when living, labored so ably and conscientiously to honor the Commonwealth of which he was a Senatorial representative. Governor Taylor was accorded the closest attention while he delivered the following graceful utterance:

MR. CHAIRMAN, LADIES, AND GENTLEMEN: I come to drop a flower of love and reverence on the grave of ISHAM G. HARRIS in the name of the State which he served so long and so well. If all the noble deeds he has done for his country and his fellow-man were flowers I could gather a million roses from the hearts of Tennesseans to-night. Whatever else may be said of him, he was an honest man. His heart was the temple of truth and his lips were its oracles. He loved his native land, and loyalty to the public duty was his creed. He lived a long and stormy life; he died a hero.

The summons came to him in the triumphant hour of the State, when the centennial bells were ringing out the old century and ringing in the new. In the glorious noontide of Tennessee's joyful jubilee, when the trumpets of peace were pouring out the soul of music on the summer air, he heard the solemn call of another trumpet, which drowned all the melodies of this world. He saw the shadow of an invisible wing sweep across his pillow, a pallor came over his face, his heart forgot to beat; there was only a gasp, a sigh, a whispered " I am tired," and tired eyelids were drawn like purple curtains over tired eyes; tired lips were closed forever; tired hands were folded on a motionless breast. The mystery of life was veiled in the mystery of death.

What is life? What is death? To-day we hear a bird singing in the tree top; they tell us that is life. To-morrow the bird lies cold and stiff at the root of the tree. It will sing its song no more. They tell us that is death. A babe is born into the world. It opens its glad eyes to the light of day and smiles in the face of its loving mother. They tell us that is life. The child wanders from the cradle into the sweet fairyland of youth and dreams among its flowers. But soon youth wakes into manhood and his soul is afire with ambition. He rushes into the struggles of real life and wins his way from the log cabin to the gubernatorial chair. The lightnings begin to leap from the gathering clouds of war; the live thunders begin to fall around him, but he stands like a lion at his post, and when the dreadful shock at Shiloh comes, where the flower of Tennessee are rushing to glory and the grave, through the rifted smoke I see him kneeling on the bloody field with the peerless Albert Sidney Johnston dying in his arms.

At last his flag goes down in blood and tears. He is exiled from his country, but the clouds soon clear away and he returns in triumph, to be clothed by the people with greater power than ever before, and to sit like an uncrowned king in the highest council of the nation, until his raven locks turn white as snow.

But the scene shifts again, and as we are called from our rev-
elry to stand around the coffin of our matchless Senator, there
are tear stains on the cheeks of merriment, and mourning muffles
mirth. They tell us that is death!

The song of the bird is the soul of melody, and the laughter
of the child is the melody of the soul. The joys of youth are
the blossoms of hope; manhood gathers the golden fruits. But
death robs the bird of its song and steals laughter from the lips
of childhood. Death plucks the blossoms of youth and turns
the golden fruits of manhood to ashes on the lips of age.

Poor bird, is there no brighter clime, where thy sweet spirit
shall sing forever in the tree of life? Poor child, is there no
better world, where thy soul shall wake and smile in the face of
God? Poor old tired man, is it all of life to live? Is it all of
death to die? Is there not a heaven where thy tottering age
shall find immortal youth and where immortal life shall glorify
thy face? It must be so; it must be so.

> A solemn murmur in the soul
> Tells of a world to be,
> As travelers hear the billows roll
> Before they reach the sea.

There must be a God. We look up through the telescope
into the blue infinite and catch glimpses of his glory. We see
millions of suns flaming like archangels on the frontier of stel-
lar space. And still beyond we see on ten thousand fields of
light crowns and shields of spiral wreaths of stars, islands, and
continents of suns floating on boundless opal seas. And are
there no worlds like ours wheeling around those suns? Are
there no eyes but ours to see those floods of light? Are there
no sails on those far-away summer seas? No wings to cleave
that crystal air?

Surely there can not be a universe of suns without a universe
of worlds, and reason teaches us that there can not be a universe
of worlds destitute of life.

We turn from the telescope and look down through the
microscope and it reveals in a single drop of water a tiny
world teeming with animal life, with forms as perfect as the

human body yet invisible to the naked eye. It can not be denied that some power beyond this world created them. We know that some power beyond this world created us. We know that they must perish and that we must die, and we know that the power which created them and us and the stars above us lives on forever.

Therefore, somewhere beyond this world there is infinite power and eternal life. Let us hope that Christ who whispered "Peace" to the troubled waters of Galilee has whispered "Peace" to the troubled soul of our departed Senator, and that his tired eyes have opened to the light of a blissful immortality.

"One sweetly solemn thought" was the offering of the memorial choir at the conclusion of Governor Taylor's address. Senator Bate, when the singing was at an end, presented Hon. John Sharp Williams, a member of Congress from the Fifth district of Mississippi, who had been invited to represent the National House of Representatives on this occasion. Mr. Williams delivered the following address:

MR. CHAIRMAN, LADIES, AND GENTLEMEN: Perhaps the best definition of philosophy is this, that it is the contemplation of death. This means in its utmost analysis that it is the study of the immutable and eternal in thought—in a word, of the immortal in man—of that which remains as characteristic and as establishing identity after what we call death has taken place.

How far death puts an end to the man as we have known him in life will always remain a debated question. Some of us, drawing a lesson from the acorn, the grain of corn, the pollen in the lily cup, the tiniest material thing that is made, can not conceive of a moment at which the essential man has ceased to exist, or his identity has been destroyed. But however skeptical the most skeptical and materialistic man who differs from us may be, there is one sense in which he must recognize the fact of the immortality of all men. It is the sense in which the man's thought and feeling, his psychical identity, continues with and influences others after his death, and often without conscious knowledge on the part of those influenced of the source whence the mental and moral molding comes.

In that phase of man's many-sided existence on this earth which we call the "public" phase—in the field of political life, where the opinions the most are molded and shaped to the governance of all—no man in Tennessee, except Andrew Jackson alone, ever influenced other men more during life than ISHAM G. HARRIS, nor will continue after death to influence them more.

There was a reason for it. It ought not to be far to seek. His position was never doubtful; his voice was never uncertain.

The man did not know what insincerity and half-heartedness were, except in so far as he observed in the lives of others the overt acts which proved them to exist.

Before I discuss the philosophy of his life, in the meaning of my definition, let me run briefly over its events.

He began life as a man when he was a child of 14. He has himself told me of incidents which show him to have been, even at that early age, the trusted and controlling adviser of his own father, suggesting and executing the family movements, ordering and prescribing its practical life. Before he was 19 he was merchandising successfully on his own account among strangers to himself and his family. He not only succeeded as a "business man," but succeeded brilliantly, and when misfortune came—a bank breaking and sweeping away an accumulated competency—the uncomplaining persistency of the boy—father here, as always, to the man—enabled him at once to meet all liabilities and retrieve all losses and lost gains. More than that, undisturbed by misfortune, marred by disaster, he executed his closely nursed desire to study and practice law. The exigencies of his business did not interfere with the execution of his purpose, nor did his study of the law interfere with his determination to make a success of his money making to the limit of becoming independent. He was never a lover of money for its own sake, agreeing with Burns that he wanted money—

> Not for to hide it in a hedge,
> Not for a train attendant,
> But for the glorious privilege
> Of being independent.

Yet thus early in life he showed his ability to make it, if he chose. Many so-called "business men"—fellows who think that God made men that men might make money—oblivious of this episode of his life, criticising Governor HARRIS'S position on a great public question, have said deprecatingly: "Oh, he is a politician; he is not a business man." There are only two mistakes in the criticism: first, the assumption—the innuendo is false, it is not true it is eternally false, that a man must have devoted his life to piling up money for himself before he can be presumed to comprehend the science of money in its relations to trade, values, and the public good; and, secondly, the politician, in this particular case at any rate, did possess all the insight, practical sagacity, and organizing methods of the typical business man. Had he chosen to remain in that walk of life and to make the accumulation of dollars his life work, he would have distanced his critics.

ENTRY INTO POLITICS.

Not only did he begin man's work in private life when almost a child, but he had taken a place in public life when almost a boy. As early as 1847, when comparatively a young man, he was elected a member of your legislature. The manner of his entrance into public life was characteristic of the man, with whom initiative was never wanting and with whom aggression frequently mounted to the level of audacity. A Gordian knot in practical politics was to be untied. Like Alexander, he cut it. A Whig and two Democrats, each of the latter jealous of the other's preferment and insistent on the maintenance of his own prestige, were candidates in a district Democratic by a close vote. To add another Democratic candidate to the list would seem the acme of folly, resulting in "confusion worse confounded," but that is precisely what ISHAM G. HARRIS advised and did, proving then, as he did so frequently in later life on battlefield and in council, that he possessed that rarest of all gifts among leaders of men, whether in peace or in war, the sagacity to know when to be audacious. As Johnson says—

When desperate ills demand a speedy cure,
Distrust is cowardice, and prudence folly.

I shall not give you in detail a history of the man's career. Suffice it to say, he became from that time on a trusted counselor in party life. In 1849 he went to Congress; remained two terms; refused a proffered nomination for a third. There was perhaps a reason for this course not at that time perfectly clear even to him. It was a day of compromise and diplomacy, when good men on both sides were striving to forestall foreseen calamities—to avoid the humanly unavoidable—disunion and war. This young man, then only 30 years of age, was not then, nor indeed at any time of his life, even when old age had mellowed him much, fitted to shine when compromise was the goal of leaders and the wish of followers. He thought, to be sure, that everything possible in that direction ought to be tried, and hence gave his voice to the experiment. But between the lines it was soon easily to be seen that this decisive and incisive intellect had no confidence in conciliatory makeshifts, however patriotically intended, but would be found when the time came with those who, like Yancey on one side and Seward on the other, announced themselves openly as being "in line of battle" for "the inevitable conflict"—to them plainly, recognizably inevitable. Until other men saw how "coming events cast their shadows before," his best place was in private life. He had no useful place in public life.

In 1856, when nominated as Presidential elector, he began to speak out the thought which had become clear in him. It was then that he took the at that time bold position for practical politics that the Union was a mere means to an end, a contrivance of our forefathers to secure the liberties and lives and protect the property of the people; that when it ceased to subserve those ends, or either of them, much more when it became a threat to the least of them, it was time to cease to regard it with superstitious awe and to seek to substitute for the means which had failed some other and adequate means. In a word, he was enlisted as a disciple of John C. Calhoun, driving his theories of right to their irresistible conclusion in action. Nor did he, foreseeing the possible issue, dread it as an alternative.

Among all the disciples of John C. Calhoun there has never been one who was better fitted by boldness of temperament, logical directness and sympathy of intellect to carry his theories unswervingly to their practical necessary, and unavoidable conclusions of fact. Long after these theories had been shattered on the battlefield, during the Fifty-fourth Congress, Governor HARRIS, speaking of the public men with whom his long career had made him acquainted as factors in political thought and work, brushing the other men whom we had been discussing aside as, after all of small estimate said: "But the greatest mind and the greatest man political life has ever furnished was John C. Calhoun." Such was his estimate of the great logician, the great apostle of State rights and local self-government.

HARRIS IN HISTORY.

But to pass on.

History was made rapidly in those days. In 1857 ISHAM G. HARRIS became chief executive of this great Commonwealth. In 1859 and 1861 he succeeded himself. Those of us who love him best like to call him "Governor" yet. He was the last of the "war governors." Nothing but the fear of the charge of invidiousness prevents me from saying that he was, in executive ability, the greatest of them all.

The Confederacy rose and fell.

A few years of exile, and in 1867 he returned to his home town and practiced law among you until 1876. From 1876 to the day of his death he was a Senator in the Congress of the United States.

I have given this bird's-eye view of a career familiar to you all, in order that you and I both might realize how long Governor HARRIS has been a moving factor, how long a leader, in American politics and during what troublous times. For these were the days that stirred men's passions and tried men's souls; first the days of antislavery agitation, the first sounds of which had alarmed Jefferson "like a fire bell in the night;" then the days of civil strife, when more than Greek met more than Greek in the fearful sweat and tug of war, and then, most trying of all, the days of reconstruction, when the very groundwork of civilization itself seemed undermined, when day after

day Southern manhood was humiliated and Southern womanhood was menaced.

Think of it! This man whose memory we celebrate to-day
saw almost the birth and saw the end of the greatest constitutional agitation the world ever saw. His public life was as
long as the natural lives of two full generations. It lapped
over in many cases to the third. I know of an instance where
he served in Congress with the grandfather, afterwards discussed the constitutional right of peaceable secession with the
father, to whom he subsequently issued a commission as a
Confederate officer, and then, long after, served with one of the
present representatives of the family once more in the Congress
of the United States. There are many families in Tennessee
with whom he has been similarly associated in public life.

But why do I wish you to realize the length and variousness
of his public service? Because, during all that long period,
this man was never once lacking in thought, feeling, utterance,
or service to the common people, nor to the State of Tennessee,
nor to the South. Because, most remarkable of all, during all
that long time, amid all the entanglements of practical politics—
and it brings strange bedfellows—no man ever so much as
claimed that this man had broken his plighted faith or been
lacking in service to any friend who had not first been notori-
ously untrue to himself. Because, during all these generations,
his enemy never accused him to another enemy of a misstatement
of fact or of a deception, and for the simplest of all reasons—the
other enemy would not have believed him.

No man was ever more soundly hated than ISHAM G. HARRIS,
and he was himself what Samuel Johnson called a "good
hater," and yet no man's word was ever more implicitly and
universally accepted as final in a statement of fact. Those who
knew him, therefore, were not astonished when, in the city of
Washington, a bitter Republican Senator from a New England
State rose to his feet when a bill was pending for the payment
of a very important claim against the Government and, ad-
dressing the Senate, the following conversation, substantially,
occurred:

"Mr President, I would like to ask the senior Senator from Tennessee a question. Has the Senator from Tennessee made a personal investigation of this case?"

Senator HARRIS replied: "I have."

"Is it the opinion of the Senator from Tennessee that this claim is just and ought to be paid?"

Senator HARRIS replied: "It is."

"Then, Mr. President," said this Republican Senator, "this is sufficient for me, and will in my opinion, be sufficient for the Senate of the United States."

In all this long period, though many people thought him often wrong, and radically wrong, nobody who understood the meaning of the word ever accused him of being a demagogue; that is, of advocating a measure because it was popular, and not because he verily believed in it, or opposing a measure because it was unpopular, and not because he verily reprobated it.

HIS INTELLECTUAL POWER.

You have known men of higher intellectual powers, though not many; you have known men—many men—of greater and broader educational cultivation, but I have never known a man whose conclusions were more logically, unfalteringly, and impersonally drawn from his premises, nor one more sincerely convinced of the eternal truth—the subjective verity—of the basic principles embodied in his premises. But this logical faculty, rare and unerring as it was, was not the secret of his success nor the mainstay of his greatness. Nor was it his power of speech, though this rose at times to the level of that of the orator "born, not made"—persuading men's wills as well as convincing their judgments. After all, however, he persuaded chiefly because he was himself so thoroughly persuaded; he convinced chiefly by the emphatic utterance of the unornamented truth, his own convictions being so intensely earnest and so palpable to all men.

There were few men who equaled him in resourcefulness and in what may be called intellectual energy. He was simply untiring, setting for himself, in the seventh decade of his life, tasks from which strong youth would have shrunk. But this even was not the main secret of his power over men. Many men have possessed equal intellectual energy and have none the less fretted away their unavailing lives. Nor can you find the secret in his remarkable executive or administrative ability—''the power to organize,'' as it is called in this latter day—though as a political organizer he seemed all-seeing, aggressive, at once bold and comprehensive—practically perspicacious of the characters, motives, opinions, and surroundings of men.

The secret which we seek is to be found in his force of character, resting on the three rocks of his courage, his confidence in the common people, and his integrity; chief of all, on the integrity of the man—integrity in its etymological sense; that is to say, the ''oneness'' or ''wholeness'' of the man. His worst enemy in his fiercest moment never charged ISHAM G. HARRIS with duplicity; that is, with doubleness of purpose, or two-sidedness of utterance, or half-heartedness in action. It is the opposite of these that make a man what he was—an integer, not duplex: a whole number, not a half number; a single number, not a mixed number—in the affairs of life.

His ends were single, his means direct.

In his old age some one asked him, ''Governor, to what do you attribute your long success in practical politics?'' His reply was, ''I don't know, unless it be to the fact that I early learned the difficult art of telling the truth.'' ''Difficult'' is well said here, for although Bulwer is right when he says, ''No task is so difficult as that of systematic hypocrisy,'' yet none is more inviting to the ordinary office seeker and officeholder, none easier to enter upon. Duplicity, the all-things-to-all-men face, manner, carriage, and utterance, which is the entrance into the field of hypocrisy, is so easy in the beginning.

Governor HARRIS carried his directness of purpose and utterance so far that he did not have even what are called ''popular manners'' to help him on. The little hypocrisies of convenance even, excusable as they are held to be in the mixed associations of public life—even these he scorned to practice. When men said, ''Governor'' or ''Senator, I don't believe you remember me,''

His reply was not the usual formula "Your face is familiar but——" etc. unless indeed, the formula was the very expression of the very fact His reply was "No sir " or " No
sir I do not." His friends have heard him say these
words in this way, not once, but many times, and have seen
sensible men receive the response sensibly and many fools go of
offended.

A MARVELOUS MEMORY

He cultivated the habit of accuracy in detail to such an extent
that it was marvelous merely as a display of the mental powers
of memory His repetitions of conversations, of arguments and
of repartee drawn from his many campaigns were intended to be
in letter, word and gesture precisely as they were uttered forty
twenty and ten years before. I have heard him relate some of
these in the office of Harris, McKissick & Turley in Memphis,
and then, nearly twenty years afterwards, I have heard him re-
peat them in Washington in the same words, with the same
intonation and emphasis, and frequently with the same gestures
If he had failed verbally to italicize anything he or the other
interlocutor had emphasized thirty years ago, I think he would
have held himself guilty of an untruth.

This integrity of character, this thing of being an integer and
not duplex, of being one—a whole number, and not a half number, nor a mixed number—stood him in much need in sore time
It stood him in need in business affairs in the hard days right
after the war. When the war came he had accumulated over
$150,000. When it ended he had absolutely nothing. I do
not suppose he ever saw the week from that time until his
death, or perhaps a few years prior thereto, when he was not
embarrassed about ready money, especially small sums, and yet
here in Memphis, or elsewhere among men who knew him, he
could borrow any sum he was willing to promise to repay from
moneyed men with whom "business was business" and not sentiment. The deposit of a policy upon his life secured them in
case of his death, and his noted integrity of character secured
them in case he lived.

Next to the fact of having mastered " the difficult art of telling the truth," the secret of the man's leadership consisted in his courage. It was this courage that gave him decision, so that he spent little time in doubting and none at all in complaining. The "whining yelp of complaint," as some one has called it, was foreign to his soul, so foreign that I doubt if the man of you all best acquainted with him can fit the expression of complaint to his countenance or imagine it modulating his voice. He was no Hamlet to have the "native hue of resolution sicklied o'er with the pale cast of thought." He never spent time soliloquizing about "taking up arms against a sea of trouble." He simply took them up.

Hence it was that when old issues were dead he promptly turned around to face new ones. The old ones he not only ceased to talk about, save as one talks of the Wars of the Roses, but he seemed to cease even to think about them, except in the historical or reminiscent way. I do not mean by that, of course, that truth and right ever ceased to be truth and right with him, no matter on which side the banner of might was unfurled. But his mind was above all things a practical mind, and the aspiration or desire or intention which was demonstrated impossible of consummation had with him practically ceased to exist.

You will remember how the Confederate cause was ingrained part and parcel of the man and how he became part and parcel of the cause, giving to it everything he had or could control except the sacred fund of posterity, the Tennessee school fund. He never any more doubted on the day of his death than he did on the day of Shiloh that the eleven States of the South had a legal and constitutional right to do what they attempted to do—peaceably to dissolve their relations with the other States in the Union—but when the people of the balance of the formerly United States had exercised their extraconstitutional "right of revolution," and our Government, rightfully or wrongfully, had become "changed, altered, and modified," he turned his face squarely about in another direction. "The stars in their course had fought against Sisera," and that was sufficient.

BELIEVED IN SECESSION

I have said that his means were direct, but that he was practical and resourceful, and hence he was no stickler about the words in which other people should express themselves when ready to join in the attainment of his end. For instance he was a believer in the doctrine of secession while many others did not believe that the right existed under the Constitution but believed in what was called the "right of revolution" the right to "change, alter, and modify" a form of government on the theory that "all just government proceeds from the consent of the governed." "Call it what you please," reasoned ISHAM G. HARRIS; "the only difference is that we go out of the Union under your theory with the recognition upon our part of the fact that there is a halter legally around our necks. In case of our failure the enemy can put one there anyhow—constitutionally or unconstitutionally. It will be the same thing to us, I imagine, whether we recognize its legal right to be there or not." Of course, you will understand that I am not giving his words, but I am expressing in my own way many words and acts of his, as I understand them, condensed into a sentence. As a consequence of this practical, nontechnical trait of the man, Tennessee did not "secede," but "declared her independence." Conceding the means, he attained the end. The two roads came together; what difference which you traveled?

As a consequence of this same practical trait, the war, when it was over, was over more completely for him than for almost any other individual in the Union. He turned to face a new war—a war begun for the preservation of civilization, and, as a means to that end, for the preservation of white supremacy in the South.

With a people placed between civilization the fruit of all the ages on one side and the written law—written with men's hands- on the other, the old "war governor," who had spent at best precious little of his time in doubt, spent now none at all in doubt, and none in doubtful utterance. Law is but the voice, government itself only the body; civilization is the essence, the spirit—the spirit of ages of progress and conquest from rude nature and ruder men—a spirit sometimes, alas! misvoiced; sometimes misembodied.

How much he had to do with that magnificent spectacle of constancy and unity, that sublime spectacle of self-mastery, as well as mastership over others, which a people subdued in battle, and from their battle purpose, but not in spirit, nor in manhood, presented to the world for ten long years; harassed, misgoverned, robbed—bearing and forbearing—waiting patiently in the leash, ready to spring whenever the opportunity for triumph came, and how much to do with the final triumph when it came, history, perhaps, will never truly tell, but you and I, resenting as he did the invitation to come down to the level of an inferior race and to "herd with narrow foreheads, ignorant of our race's gains," will, I hope, never forget.

Most of us spend 20 per cent of our time in arriving at conclusions and 10 per cent later on in reviewing them and in wondering if, after all, we may not be wrong. Half of this first 20 per cent and all of this last 10 per cent Governor HARRIS saved. After having satisfied himself that "the ends he aimed at were his country's and truth's," and therefore God's, and that they were practical of attainment, I doubt if irresolution ever cost the man five seconds of time. Andrew Jackson once said: "Take time to deliberate, but when the time for action comes, stop thinking and go in."

The two men were in many respects alike, and both possessed this advantage over common humanity, that they knew precisely and definitely what they wanted to do, and the time which others consumed in making up their minds what to do they spent in devising means to do and in doing. Goethe would have reverenced ISHAM G. HARRIS, because Goethe says: "I reverence the man who understands distinctly what he wishes to do, who unweariedly advances, who knows the means conducive to his object and can seize and use them." He also says truly that "the greater part of all the mischief in the world arises from the fact that men do not know definitely their own aims."

HIS PHYSICAL BRAVERY.

You need not be told that he was brave in battle—physically brave. The man's devotion to the truth would have told you the story of his moral courage, and his moral courage would have led you to presuppose his physical bravery. For Walter Scott was right when he said, "Without courage there can not be truth, and without truth there can not be any character." As voluntary aid-de-camp to Albert Sidney Johnston and his successors in command of the Army of the West, this governor of a sovereign State delivered messages and led regiments to the charge at Shiloh and in every engagement of that army to the close of hostilities. You will remember that he was off leading a Tennessee regiment into battle at a place so plowed with bullets that the regiment had trembled in the balance and sought the cover of a hill, when Albert Sidney Johnston was shot, and that he returned just in time to discover him wounded and to ease him off his horse to die.

I have said that the other trait of character which made him great as a leader was his confidence in the judgment of the people—in the common sense and just intentions of the common people. Even Thomas Jefferson was hardly superior to him in this respect. No man who has this democratic faith well grounded—this abiding faith in the capacity of the people to understand, provided he himself have information and ideas to communicate and ability to convey them—this abiding faith in their intention to do the right thing, when they learn what it is, can have any temptation to become that vilest of all creeping, hissing things—a demagogue. Both his own mind and his concept of what is in the mind of his hearers forbid it; they give him, on the contrary, every cause to "be just and fear not." The very groundwork of the faith of such a politician is the doctrine that if he is right he must finally be successful because the people are neither fools, to be permanently misled, nor knaves, to do the wrong intentionally.

I will be here pardoned for telling an incident from which I derived my first lesson on this subject. I was a young boy, and a just-home-from-college boy at that, with a just-home-from-college boy's contempt for the general intelligence. An estimable gentleman, whose real name I will not give, but whom I will call John Smith, was discussing with Governor HARRIS a local Democratic platform recently promulgated. Governor HARRIS was regretting that in order to fall in with a foolish and passing sentiment the platform had temporized with economical falsehood. The other man replied: "Yes, Governor, you and I understand that that is all wrong, but the common people do not, and, moreover, they do not care a rap." "That is where you are mistaken, sir," thundered the old governor; "the John Smiths and the Isham G. Harrises of this world—the so-called 'leaders' in public life—may not always be relied on to vote what is right, even when they understand it, because they have, or perhaps may have, their own 'axes to grind,' private ambitions as well as public purposes to serve; but no man who knows the common people would charge them with that crime. They have no axes except the public ax to grind; no motive to guide them in politics except the motive to ascertain what will be for 'the greatest good of the greatest number,' which is their own greatest good, and, having ascertained it, to consummate it." These are almost his very words, though it is more than twenty years since I heard them uttered. They are words of eternal truth that lead to a blessed optimism and to a restful confidence in the permanency and triumph of democracy! Words which foreshadow disappointment to the prevalent and fashionable pessimism which would despair of the Republic!

LESSON OF HIS LIFE.

I began by saying that the spirits of men abide after them immortally even on this earth in the influence which has radiated from them, becoming year by year less traceable to its origin, but broader and broader in its concentric circles. This man's life will leave, has left, among you perpetual reenforcement to several great truths—reminders priceless in value right now. Chiefly this: That a politician need not, in order to win and keep the people's favor, be either a moral coward, a hypocrite or a liar, in a word, need not be a demagogue—the epitome or brief summary of all three.

You see demagogues succeeding temporarily. You see a few of them on small arenas succeeding for a lifetime by living a lifetime lie, but it is a blessed thing to know that even in the worst days of popular government no man need be one of them and that in days of emergency no man can be one of them and succeed. It is a blessed truth that the people hate fawners and flatterers—duplex characters—that they love men—strong honest, frank, single minded men—and that all the great leaders of the people under popular governments from the beginning until now—great leaders, I say, with the element of permanency in their leadership—have been men who, like ISHAM G. HARRIS, have "learned the difficult art of telling the people the truth"—not always saints—far from it, I am sorry to say; but at least the men with "souls of fire," who lived the truth and hated a lie.

Here was a man who would neither "follow after a multitude to do evil," nor, on the other hand—worse fault yet and far more prevalent—surrender conviction while he "crooked the pregnant hinges of the knee where thrift might follow fawning" on the rich and great of this world.

Was it any wonder, then—that rare spectacle which some of us witnessed not many days ago in Washington—that spectacle which told the story in a single scene of our being the greatest and most remarkable people on the face of the globe?

Thirty years after ISHAM G. HARRIS had returned to his native State from foreign lands, where he had been an exile with a price set on his head, his body laid in state in the Senate Chamber of the Capitol of the United States. The old rebel war governor there in his coffin! Secession, civil war, and the bitter scenes and bitterer words of a stirring life forgotten by all! Only his integrity and ability and courage and love for the people remained! Around him stood grouped his fellow-Senators, among whom he had stood so long acknowledged easily chief as a parliamentarian and easily an equal in so many respects. Around him Senators and Representatives, and, rare if not unprecedented honor, the President of the United States and his Cabinet.

They did well to pay him especial and unusual honor, and you do well to honor his memory now and always.

Tennessee—proud volunteer Commonwealth—second to no State in this broad Union in resources or in men—great in everything which material nature can give, but greater yet in the memory of the achievements of her "buried warlike and her wise," will place him side by side with the greatest of them all, nor fear a just comparison with any.

Mr. SIMS. Mr. Speaker, I ask unanimous consent that my colleague, Colonel Cox, may have inserted in the RECORD some remarks upon the life, character, and services of the late Senator HARRIS. Colonel Cox is unavoidably detained at the present time.

The SPEAKER pro tempore (Mr. McMillin). Several other members have asked the same privilege, and if there is no objection, permission will be given to them all. [After a pause.] The Chair hears no objection.

Mr. CARMACK. Mr. Speaker, I ask unanimous consent that I may have printed as a part of my remarks the addresses at the memorial services of the late Senator HARRIS at Memphis.

The SPEAKER pro tempore. Is there objection to the request of the gentleman from Tennessee? [After a pause.] The Chair hears none.

Mr. RICHARDSON. Mr. Speaker, I move the adoption of the resolutions.

The resolutions were adopted; and then (at 4 o'clock and 32 minutes), in accordance with the resolutions, the House adjourned until Monday at 12 o'clock noon.

ADDRESS OF MR. COX.

Mr. Cox. Mr. Speaker, by the kindness of the House, in my absence I was permitted to place in the RECORD my humble appreciation of the public service and usefulness to the people of Senator HARRIS.

My acquaintance with him commenced at that time of my life when I cast my first vote, which was for him for governor of Tennessee. I knew him in war and in peace. I knew him as a statesman and a soldier. I knew him when a friend, and understood him when an enemy. As a man, like the most of our great men, he commenced with his common countrymen.

He learned first the duty of a citizen, and then labored to advance and protect the common welfare and liberty of his people. He was with all absolutely frank, firm, and positive. No man was ever deceived by him. He decided but once on any subject, and then never ceased to carry his convictions into practical execution. A devoted friend, a bold, daring fighting opponent, his very make-up hated deception. His very soul despised a luke-warm friend, and his very nature combated opposition. Avarice had no place in his nature. He spent his life for the State and died poor.

No stain of dishonesty is on his record, and no treachery ever even suspected. Firm, decisive, resolute, able, honest, and brave, these were the elements of his greatness. In politics a Democrat of the old school. The State had his affection; and as a protector of the rights of the States he stood at the front in all his public career. As a Democrat, he adhered to the strictest economy and left as far as possible the individual to govern himself and to be individually responsible for his own conduct. Every right under the law was equal with him; every protection given by law should operate for all alike.

No fear of the mighty and great; no oppressing the poor and needy. The public funds under his control were sacred for the objects intended. The demoralization of war and disruption of society had no effect on his integrity. He defended the funds of the people from thieves and marauders in time of peace, and in time of war carried the sacred funds of our common schools through camps, battles, and marches; and, although an exile himself, with a price set on his head, he returned every dollar to its place without the loss of a cent. What a contrast with the thieves who seized it after such honesty and stole the entire trust from our children! Indeed, such honesty as Senator HARRIS displayed is noble and grand.

I knew him in war. The first commission I ever held in the army was signed by him. I saw him a commander in chief of Tennessee soldiers. Uneducated in military affairs, yet he seemed to grasp the full and extended scope of his duties. Kind yet firm with his troops, they loved him. Without fear, they admired him, and, full of energy and self-control, he won justly for himself the great title of "war governor of the South "

What a scene it was when this great governor lifted from his horse the dying genius of war, Gen. Albert Sidney Johnston, whom President Davis pronounced the greatest of all his generals, at the terrible battle of Shiloh. I have often heard the old Senator talk of this incident, and it seemed to arouse every emotion in his true, honest soul.

A volume could be written of interesting episodes in his life—his contest for governor with John Netherland. The good joker, genial humorist, was a power on the stump. The keen, decisive logic and clear expression of thought HARRIS had were equal to the occasion.

He found in Robert Hatton a competitor worthy of any man Logical learned generous, and brave, he was ready for the lance of his competitor. Senator HARRIS always regarded Hatton as the strongest competitor he ever met. Both are gone General Hatton fell on the field of battle and rests with the dead who fell in a cause he and Senator HARRIS loved so much

Tennessee is proud of her sons, and she has been fortunate in the honor her sons have reflected on her name.

She has had her warriors as renowned as any this great Republic ever produced, and the world can not show any great soldiers Tennessee has furnished the United States many orators and statesmen. Their history is woven into the history of our common country. Among all these the late Senator HARRIS forced himself to the front. No man probably lived in Tennessee who more effectually impressed his views upon our people, and did so for their own good. He will not die. He will live in spite of death; his great efforts will tell on children yet unborn, and his virtues live as long as we have a record.

No man commanded more respect in the United States Senate than did Senator HARRIS. No Senator could misunderstand him, and he was acknowledged to be the best presiding officer of that body.

We were engaged in this House in paying respect to another sterling old-school Democrat, Judge Holman, who had been taken away. His praise was being sounded by true friends, and almost in hearing of the same the spirit of Senator ISHAM GREEN HARRIS took its eternal flight. Two great men! Two good men Two honest men, and as noble Democrats as ever defended the doctrine of the party!

I pray that in our country's history and in the defense of republican institutions young men may rise as loyal to duty and as devoted to country as the late Senator HARRIS.

ADDRESS OF MR. KING.

Mr. KING. Mr. Speaker, as a representative of the youngest State in the Union I feel honored in having this opportunity of testifying to the greatness of Senator HARRIS. The last star added to the constellation forming our imperishable Union shines this day with subdued luster and its citizens join in the universal grief expressed by the people of the United States as the memorial services of this representative body recall the death of a great American and the heroic life of one who, though dead, so entwined himself in the woof and warp of our national existence that he still lives.

The American people are not hero worshipers, but they are proud of the achievements of their countrymen, and follow with eager and anxious gaze those who may climb the dizzy heights that mark the way to glory and immortality. While the American people love the State which gives them birth, they regard with interest and affection persons from different sections who have been important factors in the country's growth, and who, by their illustrious lives, have brought renown not only to native State but to States united. They are jealous of their States and everything affecting the latter's welfare, but all lines are forgotten in the fellowship extended to those whose genius and worth have raised them to commanding heights.

The American who adds glory to Tennessee, or Maine, or California, and whose place of birth, because of valorous deeds, becomes a sacred spot, bequeaths an inheritance to every State and a patrimony to all his countrymen. The affectionate regard which comes to one (whose achievements have made him illustrious) from the citizens of his State becomes the fountain of

the mighty stream fed from every section which sweeps on in
its resistless course freighted with the loyal devotion of the citizens of the Republic. So I feel that the life and fame of ISHAM
G. HARRIS belonged not to Tennessee alone, but in part to the
State from which I come, though the Stars and Stripes was not
its ensign until years after he had been given to our country.

My personal acquaintance with Senator HARRIS was limited.
I met him but a few times, but in those few meetings I learned
something of his greatness and many of his virtues. I met him
for the first time in this building, during the winter of 1891-'92.
A measure was then pending in Congress aiming at the disfran-
chisement of my coreligionists. To protest against its enactment was the purpose of my visit here. He listened to the
importunities that he interpose to avert the impending danger.
He regarded the proposition as repugnant, and declared that no
American citizen should suffer the pains and penalties of disfran-
chisement if he could prevent it.

The constitutional aspect of the case was dwelt upon by him
with remarkable clearness. This and other questions involving
constitutional limitations and the domain of the Federal Government were discussed by him in that incisive, epigrammatic,
resistless manner which made him so powerful an ally and so
formidable a foe. He was devoted to the Constitution. It was
the anchor to his political career.

Every governmental measure and political question was determined by it. To him it was a living oracle. It was a sacred
Ark of the Covenant, not to be profaned by impious hands. A
perfunctory allegiance was not yielded by him to the sacred
principles which it guarded. Freedom and constitutional government, the dream of martyrs and patriots of the past, had been
realized, he felt, in the Republic founded by our fathers.

The preservation of this inestimable blessing was regarded by him as the chief object of life. If he had a creed, it was written by Jefferson, and its articles prescribed, not by a council of theologians, but that immortal one over whose solemn deliberations presided Washington, the greatest American. They were to him a constant source of inspiration, and his political footsteps he sought to guide by their overshadowing light.

He denied the oft-reiterated charge that there can be no national growth and progress if the Constitution of the United States is invoked against policies and measures approved and championed by the people, and for the enforcement of which an apparent necessity exists. He saw the perilous seas upon which nations have been wrecked and the dangerous channels which governments have threaded. The lesson which history teaches, that the efforts of patriots have been to establish governments limiting the power of those who govern and to prevent oppressions born of tyrannous desires of the human heart, was learned by him early in life.

The Constitution was his chart and his compass; not his alone, but the nation's; and he felt that there could be national safety and liberty perpetuated only so long as the ship of state inflexibly and undeviatingly followed that course pointed by the chart and compass. Progress to him was only made when the path of safety was followed. A prosperous, progressive, puissant country he believed could only be realized by battering down the obstructions interposed by bureaucracy and concentrated power and wealth; and the débris of monarchical institutions and the barriers, restrictions, and manacles which result from centralized power must be cleared away with invincible courage before the hosts of freedom can march on to victorious conquests in the political, industrial, and intellectual domains.

Progress and national growth did not mean to him national

power and national surveillance of the individual conduct. These were the cloaks under which the gyves of servitude were fastened upon the people. He was conservative in that he desired the triumph of natural law and the avoidance of the dangers which had destroyed nations. He was progressive in recognizing that there is a power in man which leads by evolutionary methods to higher activities and when untrammeled by unnatural laws and improper legislation, propels states and peoples with giant strides from darkness into increasing light, from industrial, political, and ecclesiastical servitude into that perfect day of freedom where the mind and body and soul possess the fruition of all labors.

He believed that political emancipation and industrial development result not from laws and statutes and penal provisions and courts and judges, but flow from that government which makes each man a sovereign and stretches forth its hand only to repress the lawless and restrain the vicious. That is not the progressive nation which controls every utility, legislates to direct every activity, and intrudes itself into every path and avenue and into every heart and brain. That is the progressive nation which points to the great unexplored and inexhaustible fields of truth, of knowledge, of wealth, and bids each person godspeed in the effort unrestrained and unrestricted so long as the right of each to continue the race is not invaded to enrich himself from the illimitable products of a bounteous harvest.

There was no dissimulation in his nature. Something of Washington's seriousness and Jackson's determination were revealed in his life. He had Dr. Johnson's bluntness, though not his cynicism. He only traveled one road at a time. He never attempted two victories simultaneously. He asked no quarter and gave none but was generous to a vanquished foe and loyal to every friend. He never reasoned in a circle.

There was only one way between given points, and that was the shortest way. There was nothing of compromise in his character. With him there could be no bartering of principle. no trafficking in truth. No doubt ever existed as to his position upon every public question. He had the sincerity of Cromwell, without the latter's devoutness.

Measured by Carlyle's standard of what constitutes greatness, Senator HARRIS was transcendently great. Sincerity, Carlyle declares, is the chief fact about a man. That person is truly great who sincerely, earnestly, faithfully lives his life no matter his calling or station, no matter what the world may say of him. If to him life has a meaning, a duty, an overwhelming responsibility, and with unfaltering courage he sincerely strives to perform it, his life becomes an epic. and though spurned by or unknown of the world, that life is a divine contribution to the uplifting of humanity.

Though unknown to the world, the example of his life is more than a sweet perfume, stealing into the materialism of our lives, a benediction that brings peace to rebellious hearts; it is a potential force acting upon the very groundwork of society for the advancement of the human family. But few men may know of him; his fame may die when he dies; but, nevertheless, measured in the great scales of the Divine One, he is a great man.

The great men of the world, those who have moved nations and have been potential for good, were those who were sincere, who earnestly struggled for the triumph of the principles which they represented. It were better to be mistaken, it were better to fall oftentimes and to stumble haltingly by the way until renewed strength and courage be gathered, and, Antæus-like, rise from the earth to fight on for what the heart and conscience demand, than to be so purposeless and forceless as to passively witness life's sanguinary conflict. Some men are so vacillating that they accomplish nothing, others so invincible in their purposes that they seem like a Nemesis.

They are like the storm; and the stupendous forces of nature seem to be raging in and about them. Like the rugged cliffs with bared heads they meet the tempest's roars, and are unshaken by the storms upon life's ocean.

Such a man was ISHAM G. HARRIS. He was a sincere, forceful, irresistible man. He was sincere, rugged, honest; whenever he believed anything to be right, he tirelessly and courageously walked in that pathway until he had achieved that which his conscience demanded of him.

There is only one dynasty, and that is the dynasty of genius—the dynasty of great men. Dynasties of men pass away, the lineage is destroyed, and the links in the great chain are broken; but the dynasty of great men will live on so long as this world moves, and in that dynasty will be found the name of ISHAM G. HARRIS. Only a few men can tread the glittering heights that lead to success; and some of us below, gazing aloft at the perilous heights which great men scale, oftentimes are timid lest they fall from precipices to destruction.

But where genius, honesty, and sincerity control there is no misstep, no faltering. He goes on, passing from the clouds to the heights beyond, where, if we can gaze with undimmed vision, we see him standing like a proud, glorious archangel in the heavens above. We know that he who surpasses or subdues mankind must look down on the hate of them below. ISHAM G. HARRIS pierced the clouds and reached the summit of greatness.

He exemplified the fact that greatness does not come from a great name, nor is it a legacy which man can bequeath. It is inherent. It comes from beyond. It develops not in the midst of affluent circumstances, but upon the hard rock of want, of penury, and of necessity. The hothouse plant does not thrive when it comes in contact with the rude forces of this earth. ISHAM G. HARRIS was not a hothouse plant. He had dwelt amidst the forces of the forest and the mountains, and had absorbed strength from the virgin forest and the rugged heights, like the giant, gnarled oak with its roots penetrating deep into the soil, gathering strength by the rude shocks encountered. Such a man was ISHAM G. HARRIS. This is as I read him and as I knew him.

I remember a few years ago the circumstance referred to by my distinguished friend from Missouri, when, especially in the West, the Democrats were concerned lest the party, partially wrecked by those who had accepted the views of the Republican party upon financial questions, would continue under their leadership until demoralization, if not destruction, of the party would ensue; but when it was announced that ISHAM G. HARRIS had called a convention in the city of Memphis, and that he had placed himself at the head of a movement to rescue the Democratic party from the dangers which were menacing it, we all felt that a new era was dawning and that the Democratic party would rise from its lethargic slumber, and, shaking its invincible locks, would scatter its foes as the lion disperses its assailants. We felt that ISHAM G. HARRIS, with his honesty, his force, his sincerity, and his devotion to the principles of the great party of Jefferson, would lead it out of the paths of danger, and that under his guidance it could know no defeat, but would go on and accomplish the great work which had been committed to its hands.

And that is the way that the people of the West felt. And so the name of ISHAM G. HARRIS is not confined to Tennessee or to the East; but the youngest State of the Union learned of his name of his glory and to-day testifies to his matchless worth in all his splendid achievements.

Mr. Speaker, ISHAM G. HARRIS is not dead, his influence lives and for good.

> There is no death! the stars go down
>   To rise upon some fairer shore,
> And bright in heaven's jewelled crown
>   They shine forevermore.

www.ingramcontent.com/pod-product-compliance
Lightning Source LLC
Chambersburg PA
CBHW030612040726
47497CB00008B/2946